ALEXANDER'S
DREAM

To Zu and Mel

love from

John X

ALSO BY JOHN MELMOTH

Novels
Welcome
Swanfall

Short stories
The Kingdom of Lagash
Angel

ALEXANDER'S DREAM

John Melmoth

Alexander thought, 'I know this.
I have dreamed it.'

Perigord Press, part of GunBoss Books,
3rd Floor, 207 Regent Street,
London, W1B 3HH, England
www.perigordpress.com

Thanks to Dean Fetzer of Perigord Press for all his help.

ISBN: 978-0-9929653-4-1

in memory of my amazing friend Jane

(February 1952-October 2015)

The dream

So.
Listen.
Perhaps this is where it begins…

It has been a day of miracles and wonders, even if, as Alexander suspects, there is something contrived and gimcrack about them. Even if they're scarcely more than conjuring tricks. But, all the same, he knows that on such things legends are based. On such stories immortality rests. And immortality is his goal beyond all others.

Having crossed the Hellespont in the late spring, he was the first to wade ashore when his flagship made landfall. He threw his spear as far as he could up the beach, claiming the land as his own. He did not look back. He never looked back.

He travelled first to windy, haunted Troy, where he visited the tomb of Achilles, who he claimed as an ancestor on his mother's side. His objective: to recruit the ghosts of the heroic dead to accompany him on his journey south and east. He marked the occasion by cutting his hair, anointing himself with oil and running naked around the grave mound. Well, it seemed like the right thing to do at the time.

Since then, he has been travelling this coast at the head of an army of thirty five thousand men and is exhausted. But he must never show it. He has to be first up and last to bed. He has to drink heroically night after night. And he must always be at the forefront in any skirmish.

Today, he has been paying his respects at the Didymaion.

Ignoring the protests of his generals and the pleas of Hephaestion, he made the decision to go alone, without his bodyguard. Alone and barefoot.

Like everything he does, he did it this way because the thought of doing it any other way simply never occurred to him.

He was tired when he took his first steps along the sacred way that seemed to go on forever. In accordance with custom, he approached with his head down. This irked him. He had spent months perfecting his kingly walk—back rigid, head tilted slightly back and to the left, knees high, eyes wide, scanning the horizon. It was a walk largely based on Bucephalus's high-stepping gait and he was reluctant to abandon it just when it was starting to feel natural. But, he knew that the resident god would be unlikely to tolerate such an uncompromising sense of self from a mortal in this place, even such a mortal as Alexander.

At regular intervals there were basins at which he cleansed himself, washing his hands, face and feet and wetting his hair in the icy water.

His tiredness fell away the closer he got to the temple. He noticed that the sacred way was unkempt; weeds and thistles, fragrant sage and oregano bristled between the flagstones. Out of the corners of his eyes he took in the statues of the Branchidae, the priestly caste who had guarded the shrine since the earth was first forged out of chaos. Some had been beheaded, others tipped on their sides, expressions of patrician disgust on their frozen faces.

A ditch ran alongside the sacred way but it was dry, the dust baked and cracked.

The enormous temple complex was scruffy and dilapidated and many of the buildings had collapsed in on themselves. The marble had been stripped from the pillars. Everywhere needed a good sweeping, a restorative lick of paint.

The prophetess was waiting for him by the holy of holies—a small, undistinguished stone building at the centre of the complex.

She was old enough to be his grandmother, or even his grandmother's grandmother. Her hair was matted, her face filthy, her eyes red and raw, her fingernails black and split. Round her stringy neck she wore a leather thong on which was hung a blue glass bead like an eye.

"She may be the great god's mouthpiece," he thought, "but her beard is thicker than mine. It seems that even the gods themselves can't be too picky when it comes to selecting a human conduit. Still, there's no denying that she looks the part: as mad as a box of frogs."

Her tunic was stained with food and wine and she stank of piss.

She placed an olive garland on his head. The stench of her armpits was overwhelming.

"Greetings, great Alexander."

He could hear the anxiety in her voice. He was becoming increasingly accustomed to that.

"Greetings, priestess. Greetings, old mother." In spite of the importance of the occasion, Alexander had to repress the urge to giggle.

The meeting of king and prophetess was being witnessed by dozens of local dignitaries who shuffled uncomfortably from foot to foot and tried to appear as if they were not hanging on his every word. He stood sideways on to them, so that they would remember his profile. He was conscious of the sun haloing his red hair.

Alexander understood—who better?—that theatre is at the heart of kingship. It would not do to compromise the solemnity of the moment.

"Welcome, great Alexander," she said again. Again, that quaver of anxiety.

"What message do you have for me, mother?"

"Come with me," she said and opened a door for him. He had to duck his head to enter, and kings, in his view, should never have to duck.

The incense fumes were so thick that he could hardly breathe. His eyes stung and his head swam. Oil lamps flickered but their light barely penetrated the scented smoke.

Three old priests in grubby robes were lurking in the shadows, feebly chanting the god's attributes and trying to stay awake. They smelled even worse than the prophetess, which was some achievement. She shooed them outside, clucking as if she was herding goats.

On a circular stone altar was a waist-high statue of the god, cast in bronze. The sculptor had depicted him as a *kouros* and without his lyre or bow. He was naked, triangular torso, rippling abs, beardless, his hair in the Egyptian style. But even though he was figured in the archaic manner, his arms were not held stiffly at his sides. Instead, they were outstretched, either in a gesture of welcome or to receive gifts.

Alexander experienced an unfamiliar thrill of awe. He knew that he was in the presence of something greater than himself. This was something that he almost never felt these days; not that it was something he had felt all that much in the past.

In front of the statue were several broken stones, black and glassy, which the priestess said had fallen from the sky and, consequently, possessed the most powerful magic. Alexander wondered how likely that was, but he said nothing.

Garlands of wildflowers hung around the god's neck.

"I was told the statue had been stolen generations ago."

"It is true. There used to be a golden statue here, the size of a man. But the Persians stole it when they sacked the temple and carried it off to Susa. The temple's sacred spring dried up in that moment. This is the model on which the sculptor perfected his technique. One of my ancestors hid it and paid for it with his life."

There was a pause. The statue seemed almost to breathe.

Alexander thought, "I know this. I have dreamed it."

"Do you have an offering for *Aegletes*, the light of the sun, great Alexander?" asked the prophetess.

Alexander looked momentarily irritated but then he pulled an object out of the fold in his tunic. It was a small, stylized golden horse with an arched neck and rubies for eyes. He handed it to her and she placed it at the foot of the statue. The horse's eyes winked fire in the flickering light. The bead on the prophetess's necklace glowed.

This was not the gift he had meant to give. Days ago, he had decided that a figurine from lost Atlantis would be the most appropriate offering. He had bought her in the market at Halicarnassus for a small fortune. Not much bigger than his longest finger, she was naked from the waist upwards, with a panther perched on her head and a snake in each hand. He believed her to be a primitive earth goddess. She radiated extraordinary power, which was why he had chosen her. And why he had paid for her rather than kidnapping her by right of conquest.

But somehow she had disappeared—lost or stolen—on yesterday's march. When they brought the news to him last night—the quartermasters and the stewards blaming one another—his anger had been terrible. Surely it was the worst kind of omen and there was the very real risk that the god would feel insulted by a last-minute substitute.

He sent the quartermasters and stewards back to check every step they had travelled during the day. But when they returned at dawn they had found nothing. Their faces were so marked with dread and exhaustion that he forgave them. How could he not?

"Your offering is acceptable to the god of truth and prophecy," said the crone.

Alexander shivered with relief.

And then he noticed that the old woman was changing in subtle ways. Her eyes, which had been flickering about nervously, became still and fixed on his, full of challenge. She seemed more upright, more rounded, younger, more vigorous, more certain of herself. Her voice had deepened. There was no catch of anxiety now that the god was speaking through her.

"What do you wish to ask me?" said the god.

The skin was squirming on the back of Alexander's neck; the gooseflesh erupted on his forearms. He revered but did not trust the god who, after all, had brought plague to the Greeks at Troy and was instrumental in the death of Achilles.

"I wish to know the future."

Dramatic pause. And then: "You will be Lord of Asia."

Alexander's heart was racing. Lord of Asia? And then Lord of All? Still, it doesn't do to ask for too much at one time. Mission accomplished for now.

Alexander and the priestess stood for a while contemplating the god's likeness. When she led him back outside, he saw that she was once again a skinny, frightened, stinking old harridan, possessed of an amusing range of vatic tics.

He mingled for a while with the crowd outside. "*Echete erthei poly*? Have you come far? Really, what a coincidence, I once opened a new theatre there. What do you do for a living? Do you like horses?" Feigned interest in their banalities. "From Akyaka, your Majesty, a few hours' ride away." "I deal in dried herrings from the Baltic, your Majesty." "Your Majesty, my company builds houses in Myra. I hope to welcome you there." "May I introduce my wife, your Majesty?"

He had a sense that something was about to happen. And then a voice called out, "A miracle. The sacred spring has started to flow again."

So that was it. Must have taken some organising. Whatever else, you couldn't accuse the priestess of lacking a sense of drama. It was almost too much. Again, he had to stifle the urge to laugh. Rumour buzzed through the crowd. A legend was in the process of being born.

He took his leave of the prophetess and set off alone back down the sacred way and towards camp. The visit had gone well; better than he could have hoped. The god had blessed his endeavours and the priestess's antics had ensured that today would be remembered forever.

As he walked, his eyes on his feet in the dust, he heard the sound of rushing water. He did not look back, but smiled with satisfaction when he glimpsed clear water flushing through the ditch by the side of the way.

He remembered the words of Xenophon whose *Anabasis* he kept under his pillow, along with *The Iliad*: *"A ruler should not only be greater than his subjects; he should cast a spell on them."*

He tried to look as if this was what he had been expecting; as if this sort of thing happened to him all the time.

In that moment, he decided to order the rebuilding of the temple complex on a colossal scale.

But if the day ended well, it had not begun so auspiciously.

Alexander had woken early, tormented by a dream.

He had dreamed of two boys. Two young men. Both beautiful in ways that he knew he was not; not that anyone would ever tell him so. In his dream, he and Hephaestion were walking beside a swirling river. The air was full of the sound of cicadas. Hawks flickered overhead. They were in a canyon whose walls towered over them. Alexander looked up. The first of the boys was standing on a high outcrop of rock, with the clouds boiling behind him. He was staring at something Alexander could not see. Alexander wished to befriend the boy and called to him and waved. The boy turned to wave but lost his footing. He cried out as he fell like a star and vanished.

In his dream, Alexander wanted to run to where he had fallen but something prevented him. He couldn't move from the spot.

He looked up again (as a king and as a man, he knew that he must always look up) and he saw what appeared to be a life-sized golden statue standing on the edge of the cliff. The sun glinted on its metallic surface. But as is the way with dreams, as Alexander watched, the statue warmed and turned to flesh and blood. But he couldn't see this second boy clearly. He was somehow shadowy or indistinct, as if he was standing further away. For a moment he turned to look at Alexander and their eyes met, but then he turned his gaze to the sky. He was very like the first boy and he too was looking at something Alexander couldn't see. Again Alexander wished to know him better. But he knew that if he called or waved this boy too would lose his footing and fall.

In his dream, Alexander was paralysed by indecision.

He woke with a smear of sweat on his forehead and immediately sent for Aristander, who was ushered into his presence still wiping the sleep from his own eyes.

He told the older man of his dream. Aristander thought for a moment and then said, "It is a good dream. The falling boy is you. You are falling on your enemies like a thunderbolt from the sky."

"But what about the second boy?"

"You said that he was further way. That is another part of you—*pothos,* the traveller rather than the warrior, the explorer rather than the general, the man who seeks always to cross to the other side. *He* was further off because *you* have a long way to travel before you reach the ends of the earth."

Although a rational man—he had been well schooled by Aristotle—Alexander was also profoundly superstitious. And he had always had absolute faith in Aristander who, after all, had predicted his arrival in the world.

It happened like this. Philip, Alexander's father, dreamed that he had sealed up the womb of his wife, Olympias, with a wax seal, which carried the device of a lion. Aristander argued that we don't bother to seal up empty things and that, therefore, Olympias was pregnant with a child who would be lion-like and invincible. He was right. That child was Alexander.

But, in spite of his respect for the older man's interpretative skills, Alexander had not been happy with his explanation and had asked him to think again. "Why did the second boy appear to emerge from a golden statue? I do not think that he was further away. It was just that I could not see him so well. There was something insubstantial about him."

When Aristander asked for an hour to think it over further, Alexander rather suspected that it was because he wanted his breakfast. When he returned he said, "I have given your dream much additional thought. I stand by my interpretation of the first part. You will fall upon your enemies like a bolt out of the blue. However, the second part of your dream may also have another meaning. The boy who emerges from the golden statue, the boy with his eyes on the sky, is your soul; the you that is within you. Your soul is golden because it comes from the immortal gods, because you are a king. The fact that the boy's eyes are fixed on the heavens means that he cannot be constrained by earthly boundaries. He cannot be called to earth by those who are on the ground."

Alexander smiled at the words 'also' and 'another'. But, comforting though Aristander's interpretation was, he knew that it was not right, that at best it was not the whole truth. Still, he could hardly blame him for trying to put the most positive gloss on things.

For the first time in his life, he realized that Aristander was not infallible.

This dream returned many times to haunt him during the years that remained to him. The memory of it was always with him...

Readiness

Maybe it happened like that.
Maybe it didn't.
Whatever.
But listen.
This is where it begins…
Everything is in readiness.

Elif has made the beds and folded the towels into butterfly shapes. She has sprinkled geranium petals on the counterpanes. She has scrubbed the bathroom so that the mirror and the chrome shower fittings gleam. She has emptied the bin of yesterday's used toilet paper. She has polished the kitchen sink and the work surfaces, mopped the tiled floors and swept the patio. She has persuaded the mosquito net above the double bed into an elegant helix, dusted some of the objects with which Mr Basak has decorated the place, and taken out the trash.

She has done all these things many, many times before. And she is sick of them all. Sick to death. *Gina gelmis.*

She is sweating and all the while, she has been sighing and clutching her back theatrically even though there's no one to witness her performance.

She wonders what the new guests will be like, but it probably doesn't matter. Either she will be invisible to them or they will try too hard to be friendly, not realising that she has as little interest in their lives as they do in hers. Probably less. That she is simply doing her job. Making money to supplement Urfuz's wages as an agricultural worker without land of his own. Money that will be used to ensure that her children have a better chance in life than she and Urfuz ever had. Money that means that her daughter won't have to wait on holidaymakers hand and foot. Won't have to dance attendance on people who seem comfortable spending all day in swimming costumes. Sometimes very small costumes. Sometimes very large people in very small costumes.

But don't get her started. She is afraid that she might not know where to stop. She has to accept that she doesn't understand these people. And if she keeps her opinions to herself and smiles often enough there is usually a tip at the end of the week. A tip that may mean very little to the people who give it but might be what Urfuz earns in half a week. A tip that will pay the monthly broadband bill so that the kids are not disadvantaged when they do their homework.

All that's left to do is assemble the welcome hamper. She puts a wicker basket on the table, in which she carefully arranges: a tin of black olives, a jar of honey taken from hives owned by a new cooperative in Kinzmik, a tin of Turkish coffee, a bag of pasta whirls, a packet of malted biscuits, three small tins of tuna and a jar of pasta sauce with tomatoes and aubergines. She places four small oranges and two apples in the fruit bowl. In the fridge she puts: two bottles of Turkish beer, one bottle of Turkish white wine, two large tomatoes, five small cucumbers, a lettuce, some extremely strong green chillies that she fully expects to throw out untouched at the end of the week, a chunk of a mild sheep's cheese and a large tub of yoghurt.

Two years ago a couple complained to their holiday company that the welcome hamper was 'dull' and 'insufficient'. She knows what she would do with such people in an ideal world, but she just has to smile and keep her opinions to herself.

While she has been doing this, Urfuz has been tidying the garden. He takes pleasure in this. Although the garden is not his, he feels a sense of ownership, a sense of pride in his work. After all, he has been working with Mr Basak since the beginning. Together they have created this garden out of the hillside.

He's also been attending to the pool, a job for which he has considerably less enthusiasm. He's emptied the skimmer basket and the hair and lint basket in the filtration system—pulling out handfuls of hair like scummy seaweed—and backwashed the filters. He's checked the pH and total alkalinity levels for the third time this week. He's checked the calcium, chlorine and bromine levels. He's checked for scaling and corrosion and he's added a dash of algaecide. He's lubricated the valves, O-rings and plugs in the pump's motor. He's inspected the tiles and grouting, particularly at the water line. He's tested and adjusted the oxidizer and stabliser levels. He's checked the water temperature, mopped the stone surround, topped up the water level. He's scooped out the leaves and he's hauled dozens of drowned insects out of the water, including the corpse of a large, normally reclusive, mildly venomous spider.

And he's cleared a mound of tortoise shit from the poolside.

Why would a tortoise choose that exact spot to unload itself so spectacularly? Over and over again. When he was a boy, they would have eaten such a tortoise—cooked in its shell in the ashes of the fire—without a second thought. But not any more. Mr Basak is insistent that no animals, birds or insects should be unnecessarily killed in the garden.

Even so, a few months ago, driven to distraction, Urfuz had decided to destroy it. He put it in a sack one evening when the Basaks were away from home and carried it down to the village. He'd thought of a number of ways to assassinate it—drown it in his water butt, drop it from the roof of his house, plunge a needle into its brain—but when it came to it, he found himself unable to do any of these things. Not for the sake of the tortoise, but because he couldn't rid himself of the fear, which he knew to be irrational, that Mr Basak would somehow find out. In the end, he simply released it into the fields and forgot about it. Five weeks later he discovered it once again by the side of the pool, enjoying an insouciant bowel movement, as if it had never left. Urfuz knew when he was beaten. It was obvious that the tortoise had been put on the earth in order to accustom him to life's frustrations, that this was a tortoise sent to torment him. For the moment, a fragile truce has broken out between them.

The prohibition against murder does not, of course, extend to snakes, of which there are always many. But Urfuz is under strict instructions never to kill them in sight of the guests. They might not understand.

It's different when there are no guests. Last autumn, he discovered a snake that was nearly two metres long and the thickness of a man's arm, hiding in leaf litter. Its body was grey and its head was golden. At least it was right up until the moment Mr Basak blew it off with his shotgun.

Urfuz and Mr Basak danced around the snake in triumph and

then they started to laugh and for a while it was as though they wouldn't be able to stop. When they finally did, Mr Basak invited him back to his house for a glass of fiery raki—a rare treat, which brought tears to their eyes. They toasted one another's prowess. Then he took the snake's body slung over his shoulder down to the village to show the children who laughed and jeered at it. He then chopped it into pieces and fed it to his dog and to all the cats he could find at the time.

Elif takes a final look round: everything's ready. She locks the door behind her. She'll meet the new people tomorrow by which time they will have doubtless trashed her arrangements. She stretches in the hot sun and again clasps her back.

Urfuz starts his motor scooter and she climbs on behind him, sidesaddle. They buzz slowly down the hill to the village. Urfuz has a cigarette in his mouth and the smoke from it is blowing in her face.

There will be a wedding party in the village this evening— music, dancing and food. She thinks that she will take the children if she is not too tired. She won't dance, though. She is thirty eight, after all. But she'll sit and drink tea and gossip with all the other old women. She's looking forward to disapproving of the way the young people are certain to misbehave.

The sound of Urfuz's scooter fades. All that remains is the screech of the cicadas.

The official and the English woman

Everything is in readiness…

The villa is perched on the side of a huge limestone outcrop that looms over the village like the wall of a gigantic castle. The gardens are terraced. The land drops vertiginously away. Built of wood and stone, the house seems, nevertheless, weightless. Like it's flying. Defying gravity.

To the front is a U-shaped valley of tawny fields, in which wheat, sesame and maize have been grown in strict rotation since forever.

The lower slopes of the valley are a patchwork of olive groves and orange plantations. The higher slopes are covered with a dense forest of stone pines, holm oaks and gunluks (known locally as incense or liquid amber trees). Everything melts and shifts in the heat haze.

To the west, a few kilometres away, a tinfoil sea is reflecting a blazing sky.

A short distance inland, a three kilometre-long double avenue of eucalyptus trees—eighty years old and nearly thirty metres high—marches across the valley floor from one side to the other, cutting the valley off from the sea, like a border dividing one country from another. The only gap in this line of trees is just wide enough to allow the road through, keeping open this single connection between valley and shore.

17

The trees were planted all those years ago at the instigation of an unusually farsighted official who was sent here from Istanbul to drain the malarial swamp that used to border the sea.

So successful has his scheme proved, that it is now forbidden to plant any further eucalypts in case they take even more moisture from the soil, which is starting to dry out and blow away.

If this long dead official were alive today it is likely that he would be entirely indifferent to the beauty of these magnificent trees with trunks like dinosaur legs. He was, after all, known to be a very practical man where his professional life was concerned. Not much given to flights of fancy.

He's scarcely remembered now—the trees and the reclaimed land to their seaward side are his only monument— and there's hardly anyone alive who knew him. But if his name does come up, it's loosely associated with stories of a man who, for the time he was here, lived an austere and isolated life in the hills, among the olive groves. A man who lost his wife and child, and who found consolation in his work and his studies.

He was willing to move from the culture and bustle of Istanbul to this remote province because, as well as an engineer, he was a scholar of antiquity, with a closely guarded but intense passion for archaeology.

During the week, as far as he was concerned, this was a place of work, of engineering problems, of civic responsibilities. He had been posted here to solve a problem; he would solve the problem. End of.

But at weekends and in his spare time, it was transformed into a land of myths and stories, a land once inhabited by the almost inaudible, almost forgotten Lycian civilization.

The official was very firmly of the view that the twentieth century had a lot to learn from the Lycians who, in contrast to the rest of the contemporary Hellenic world—which was characterized by centrifugular, feuding, testosterone-fuelled city states, for whom war was the normal state of affairs—showed an anachronistic talent for federation and nation building.

And, unlike his new neighbours, he had not forgotten that Alexander the Great, shining like a god, his head full of Homer, lightning flickering around him, passed this way in the late autumn of 334BC like an arrow in flight. That he travelled with his favourite seer in his retinue, a local man, Aristander of Telmessos, the city of light, which is modern day Fethiye. That he was on his way to consult the oracle at the Temple of Apollo in Didyma, with its sacred way, its towering columns and its laurel groves.

The official believed that this coast was where Alexander learnt his trade. That his conquest of this region was a young man's—he was just twenty two—dress rehearsal for the mature man's conquest of everything that lay to the east.

Although his work had been finished years before, he continued to rent a cottage in these hills until the early 1950s in order to pursue his lonely preoccupation with a dead culture. There were wolves and bears in these forests back then.

And it was in this cottage that he played host one afternoon in September 1952 to an English woman—no longer young— with a man's face and a boy's haircut and a fearless heart under her army surplus parachute silk underwear. She was a travel writer and one of the first Europeans to show any interest in this place since the mid-nineteenth century. She was sailing southwards down the coast with a man from the British consul, who was acting as both guide and chaperone. They had travelled up the hillside on hired horses (there were no roads then), which they tethered to a wooden post in the official's garden.

Like the official, the English woman seemed to have difficulty distinguishing the past from the present. For her as for him, they were co-existent. Like him, she still caught glimpses of Alexander marching in these hills at the head of his army. The official was now an old man but his passion for the place was undimmed. He and the English woman talked for hours until she and the man from the consul had to leave to rejoin their boat, which was at harbour a few kilometres away. The official was struck when she said that of all the many places she had travelled to, both on the edges of Europe and in the deserts of Arabia, this coast was the most haunted and the most magical she had ever visited. That it was a place where the dead—even the long dead—continued to make their presence felt. Where story and myth, possibility and actuality, dreams and memories all intersected. Where time behaved in disconcerting ways.

When she left, he was never able to call her name to mind.

One evening, early the following summer, he was sitting at his desk. The air was thick with the possibility of thunder. A large leather-bound book was on the reading slope in front of him. The print was so small that—even in the light of the oil lamp—he was compelled to use a magnifying glass. But tonight, unusually, he was unable to settle to his studies. The words blurred and he read the same sentence over and over without comprehension. His eyes were tired. He stood up and paced around the room before sitting once more at his desk. He lit a small black cigarette and fragrant smoke filled the room. He noticed a sudden silence. He glanced at the window and was startled to see what appeared to be two pale faces on the other side. He felt a pain in his heart. He got to his feet and walked to the window so that he could see more clearly. He smiled, waved and made a gesture of welcome, invited them in.

Kelebek Kirmizi

By the gate is a pokerwork sign burnt into a slab of pale olive wood: '*Kelebek Kirmizi*'—the red butterfly.

Everything is in readiness. Everything is waiting.

But nothing is still in the house or the garden.

The floorboards shift and creak as the temperature continues to rise throughout the afternoon. The breeze whispers through the tiny spaces between the roofing tiles. The fridge clicks and burbles. A large bubble like a jellyfish works its way up through the plastic demijohn of the water cooler with a glooping noise. The drapes tremble. Something is causing the mosquito net to shift. The light through the window moves slowly across the floor. Dust motes swirl, collide and sparkle. Infinitesimal particles settle on a piece of grey stone—carved with an egg and dart frieze—on the window ledge. As the light sweeps across the bookshelves, it briefly spotlights the authors' names on the spines: Lee Child, Sue Townsend, Ian McEwan and, surprisingly, E M Forster and D H Lawrence.

The air is so clear and the light is so strong that the ants milling about on the flagstones by the pool cast tiny perfect shadows, dragging their exact doubles with them everywhere.

There is a small island in the pool, on which Mr Basak instructed Urfuz to plant a single palm. It looks like a cartoon desert island. Each stem terminates in around forty dagger-like, dark green leaves. They move in the slightest breeze and are in a continuous process of unravelling, their bast exposed like pale string.

A black and yellow dragonfly rattles across the pool and catches sight of its reflection in the steel ladder. It batters itself against this apparent foe. Meanwhile, several smaller red ones snooze at the side of the water—heads down, tails up, wings at rest—not so easily taken in.

Large orange and yellow butterflies, named after a great queen of Egypt, cruise past. A huge black and white beetle drones in like a bomber.

A skinny cat, as grey as a ghost, with even greyer eyes and legs like stilts, slinks fastidiously from shadow to shadow. In the winter, it travels up into the mountains and lives by hunting; in summer it moves into the garden in search of an easier life, courtesy of the holiday makers who don't share the local rather uncompromising view of feral cats.

At the moment it is starving and its fur is matt and dusty. But it is as beautiful as ever. It curls against a warm wall and slips into a doze. Like Elif, it is waiting to discover what the new people will be like.

Under the eaves of the porch a predatory wasp amputates the wings of a pale moth with the precision of a psychopathic surgeon. It flies away with its victim clamped to its chest. A pale wing, scarcely there at all, rotates gently down to the ground. (What is the sound of a moth's wing striking a stone floor when there's no one there?)

The olive trees shiver expectantly—silver and dazzling. A few of the leaves have turned yellow in the early summer's heat and drop with a sound like hailstones.

Blue rock lizards duck and threaten.

An eagle with a damaged wing flies over. Seen from the ground, there are gaps where its pinion feathers should be, like missing teeth in an old comb. It utters a single piping call.

The cicadas screech and the pines creak and crack.

A blue glass, eye-shaped *nazar* or amulet has been embedded in the concrete at the threshold to the villa. It has been placed there to protect its occupants from any malign powers there might be in the area. It catches and reflects the sun's rays.

Everything is in readiness.

This is where it begins.

And...

... just maybe

... where it will end.

Gin and orange

Mrs Basak is a tall, elegant, smiley lady, beautifully dressed, a head taller than the little man with curly hair by her side, who turns out to be her husband.

"How was your flight? We were expecting you earlier."

Mum looks sad for some reason but she smiles and says, "The flight was fine, thank you, but the transfer by *dolmus* took longer than it should have. The road was blocked by around fifty cars travelling the wrong way, honking their horns and waving flags. We asked the driver what was going on but I don't think he understood us."

"It was probably a wedding. Those cars must have been going to collect the bride from her village and Turkish people do not always obey the traffic laws. They think of road signs as a matter for debate rather than something to be observed under all circumstances."

Dad says, "You speak brilliant English, Mrs Basak. Where did you learn?"

"Please call me Seyhan. My husband is Kemal. I am a little... I think you say 'rusty', but I studied languages at university and spent a year in America at the University of Illinois. But I really should practise more. We sometimes listen to the BBC World Service on the radio. My husband's English is quite good also. But he always wants to use it to discuss politics with our guests.

25

And any discussion of politics seems to make him angry and it is not so good for him to get angry. He has the high blood pressure."

As she says this, she pats her husband on the shoulder and he smiles, as if he's achieved something rather wonderful.

Mum says that the villa is lovely and the garden is also beautiful.

Mrs Basak is pleased and explains that they built the villa twelve years ago as a weekend retreat when they were living in Kinzmik because of their jobs.

"There was nothing here when we built the house and the road was so steep that all the building materials had to be brought up the hill by tractors. And even one of them fell into a ditch. We had to pay the villagers to bring the roof tiles by hand across the fields. They also had to carry our furniture. I think they thought we were mad to want to live up here. But the views are so wonderful."

She says that they moved to this area full-time about five years ago when they retired and have built another house that they live in (it doesn't have a pool) and rent this one out.

"Well," says Mum, "we're really glad that you do. It's lovely."

"Thank you. Now I'm sure you are tired and hungry after your journey, but if we could trespass on your patience for a few more minutes my husband has some points of information for you."

Mr Basak looks and sounds as though he's addressing a public meeting. "Welcome to my country…"

"Blimey," says Dad some time later when Mr Basak has

finally left, "I thought he was going to tell us where the nearest supermarket is or what to order in local restaurants. I wasn't expecting a potted history of Turkey since the Second World War. I wasn't expecting to be given his views on the rise of fundamentalism, or the importance of recycling, or the strategy of the regional government, or why Turkcy has never been admitted to the EU. And I certainly wasn't expecting a quick jaunt through the history of Lycian civilization from the sixth century BC. Fascinating though it all was. And I'm not sure that I needed to know on my first evening that Tiberius ordered the repair of the amphitheatre at Patara. Maybe that particular piece of information could have waited until tomorrow. I'm starving."

"Well," says Mum, "I liked him and was interested in what he had to say. He's clearly very proud of his country and concerned about what he sees happening to it. It's good to see someone with a passion like that... Why don't you make us a drink, while I get some food on the go?"

So, Dad and I sit at a table in the garden as the light starts to fade. Dad bought a bottle of duty free gin at airport.

"There isn't any tonic but I could use those oranges in the fruit bowl. My grandmother used to drink gin and orange on high days and holidays. Just saying the words 'gin and orange' makes me think of her lipstick and I swear I can smell her face powder."

Mum says she'd love one.

Dad cuts an orange in half and squeezes a small amount of juice into their glasses and tops them up with a large amount of gin. He says, "Cheers," and they touch glasses. He drinks. "Blimey, if I have to pour this down my throat all week I think

I'll turn into my grandmother."

On the far side of the valley, we can see the lights of another village. The air is soft and warm. Bats put on an aerial display just in front of us, swooping and swerving in complete silence.

The trees in the garden move. The cicadas fall silent.

We can hear thunder rumbling in the mountains, but the sky above us is clear. As the light fades, the stars start to appear. First a few and then more and more, and then millions and millions. A cluster of stars is hanging over the other side of the valley. It looks like a bow and arrow or a bird in flight, maybe a goose or a swan.

Mum brings out supper on bright yellow plates. It's pasta with a sauce made of tomatoes and tuna. It looks and smells delicious.

Mum has put the iPod in the docking station and music drifts out of the windows. A man with a very haunting voice is singing in German. The music sounds louder in the open air than it does indoors.

We sit here for ages until it's so dark that we can't see our hands in front of our faces. Suddenly, a bird begins to sing out of the darkness, and then another and then another, until the night air is full of birdsong. Mum is so excited.

"Nightingales. Isn't that wonderful? I haven't heard nightingales sing since I was a kid."

Even Dad looks pleased.

And now everyone is in bed.

Mum and Dad are under the mosquito net. He told her that mosquito nets are a well known aphrodisiac and that when she saw him under it she would definitely find him completely irresistible.

She said that the chances were that she wouldn't.

This is probably not the kind of conversation that parents should have in front of their children.

He told her that he's had a bit of a thing about mosquito nets ever since he saw a film set in Africa when he was at a particularly impressionable age.

"My sexuality obviously got stuck at that moment. It was a formative experience. I can't help myself."

Mum said, "I still wouldn't get your hopes up too much."

This is very *definitely* not the kind of conversation that parents should have in front of their children.

I'm in the much smaller bedroom with two single beds. There's a large photograph of a black and yellow butterfly on the shelf and a collection of sea shells. There's a small mirror and some beaten-up paperbacks. There's a clumsy wooden sculpture on the chest of drawers; I think it's meant to be a donkey. Or maybe it's an angel. There's a beautiful red and purple rug on the floor with intricate geometric patterns. For some reason there are pink petals on the bed; maybe they blew in through the window.

I'm not in the least tired. So, I sit up and lean on the sill of the open window. I can hear the trees moving. The lights on the opposite side of the valley have gone out. I can hear a car's engine in the distance. There are tiny rustlings in the garden and I can hear the whirring of the pool filter. An owl screeches somewhere. The moon is up and the swan has flown to a different part of the sky.

The blue of Heaven

I love this time of morning.

I love having the garden to myself.

And I love to think of Matt sleeping in the little room. Sleeping like a baby.

Steve didn't stir when the muezzin at the mosque in the village started to call, reminding the faithful that it was time for prayer. There was crackle of static and then this magical voice splitting the silence. I looked at my watch: six fifteen.

I poked him in the back and he said, "Certainly, Auntie Doreen, won't be a minute." I didn't think that was worth responding to.

Early as it was, when I came outside I discovered that fresh bread had already been delivered. Seyhan said that someone who worked for them—I think his name is Urfuz— would drop it off when he came to check the pool. Kemal said something about being happy to be judged by such small kindnesses. And then he went and spoiled it by saying that their aim is to offer a *total* service. I could hear the italics. Sounded like the sort of thing people say at management conferences.

I love this place.

It feels so known and so familiar. From the minute we got here, it felt like coming back to somewhere we'd been before.

It's important to keep telling myself how beautiful the world is. On the plane yesterday, I spent most of the journey looking out of the window. When we emerged above the clouds about ten minutes out of Heathrow, the sky was a brilliant blue dome that seemed to go on forever. I kept saying the word 'cerulean' to myself. Like a kind of mantra. The blue of Heaven. The blue of infinite possibilities.

When I was a kid, I was given a tin box of watercolours, the ones with the little squares of paint that you have to wet with a brush. Some of them had magical names: 'burnt umber', 'Sienna', 'Chinese white', 'ultramarine', 'cobalt blue', 'vermilion' ('cinnabar'), 'viridian' and 'cerulean blue'. Names that seemed impossibly exotic.

I was never much good at painting. Mainly I produced pictures of little square houses with curtains at the windows and a path leading to the front door. Tulips in neat flowerbeds. But I loved that paint box. Sometimes I would open the lid just to look at the names. It was like reading a wonderfully romantic story.

But it's amazing how everything comes back to bite you. A few weeks ago, there was something on TV about colour. Apparently, before the eighteenth century everything from sheeps' hooves to bulls' blood was used to produce an artist's palette.

But then, with industrialization, lots of paints were produced using new chemical processes, and the side effects could be catastrophic. Many of the colours I loved were among the worst culprits. Chinese white could result in irreparable kidney damage, chrome yellow led to fits, and cobalt blue could—quite literally—cause your heart to stop.

I would love to have a garden like this. Scarlet hibiscus; the subtler, paler oleanders. Jasmine. Olive and lemon trees. And there's a shrub that I can't identify, with orange, scarlet and purple flowers on the same stems.

When the *dolmus* brought us through the local village yesterday evening, all the gardens were bursting with spring flowers. Purple vetch and cornflowers, poppies, spires of foxgloves. Clouds of honeysuckle and hollyhocks as high as the cottage roofs; millions of roses; geraniums the size of cauliflowers; dahlias in June, for God's sake. They looked like English cottage gardens on steroids.

I think I just met Urfuz. As I was walking down towards the pool, I suddenly came a across a tiny, nut brown man (burnt umber, even) with a huge moustache. He looked scared. I wished him *guneydin*. He looked even more startled. He smiled and vanished through a screen of oleander. I guess he's had lots of practice at making himself invisible. It's probably part of the job description. Wanted: a man who can look after a pool and who is an expert at not being seen. I suppose that they think that's what we want when we come to stay. To avoid embarrassing encounters with the hired help.

There's still a light mist in the valley but I can see a few cars on the road. They seem almost to be moving in slow motion.

I think I could sit here forever. Still, I suppose I'd better give some thought to breakfast.

The world's smartest cat

While we're sitting at breakfast, a skinny grey cat comes yowling round the corner. It makes eye contact with me and doesn't blink. I immediately know it is a very wise cat. Possibly the wisest cat ever. The world's smartest cat.

To begin with, it sits a few metres away from us, mewling sadly, trying to make us feel sorry for it. But gradually it creeps nearer and tries to rub itself against Dad's leg.

"Christ," he says, "it's got some sort of skin disease. Mange or something. Urgh."

He jumps up and runs at the cat hissing. It backs off a bit but is clearly unimpressed by this performance. It looks into his eyes and continues to mewl. It's already decided that it can wait Dad out. That if it takes its time and doesn't push too hard, it will probably get what it wants.

Mum says that the poor thing is starving.

"Well, just so long as you don't feed it."

"If I don't feed it, it's going to spoil my holiday."

She goes into the house a reappears with a saucer of yoghurt and crumbled sheep's cheese.

Dad looks as though he's going to protest but he doesn't.

Mum puts the saucer on the floor. For a moment the cat stares deep into her eyes. The look on its face says that it knows

33

everything about her; her strengths and her weaknesses, her hopes and her fears, her beliefs and her suspicions. Then it rushes at the food and starts to eat.

"Maybe we can buy some cat biscuits at the supermarket," she says.

"There's obviously no point in trying to dissuade you, but I'm not sure that Turkish country people are really into cat biscuits."

The cat is finished. It curls up against the wall. It looks into my face and then Mum's and then Dad's and then back to mine. Its eyes widen and then it blinks. By now, it seems to know everything about *all* of us. It is peaceful and friendly. It won't trouble us again until the next time it is hungry. Meanwhile, it obviously feels that it might as well keep us company. Its eyes close.

Soon after breakfast has been cleared, the cleaning lady, Elif, turns up. She looks at the cat, which is asleep, snaps her fingers and says something like 'pphhhwww'. The cat opens its eyes, takes one look at her, says something like 'eeaww' and runs away down the garden, its tail flapping indignantly. Smart cat.

Elif is plump and brown with a round face. When she smiles her teeth are white and perfect. But, obviously, cats know they can't mess with her.

She's wearing baggy checked trousers like pyjamas, Crocs, a purple T shirt, a purple headscarf. Straight away, Mum starts trying to talk to her. Thanking her for the housework she hasn't done yet. Asking her about her children, even though she only speaks about four words of Turkish and Elif doesn't seem to speak any words of English.

Dad rolls his eyes and suggests a walk, if Mum can tear herself away from her 'new chum'.

The back of the villa is built into the side of the valley. There's a steep staircase leading to a rough track, which is the only way of getting here.

The hire car has been delivered during the night and is parked by the side of the track. Even though it's still early, the car's bodywork is too hot to touch.

The track leads gently uphill. On the right is a sheer rock face; on the left is a dense wood. The sea is just visible in the distance.

The trees are enormous—thirty metres tall. In many places they are growing out of bare rock, their roots visible. The tops of the trees bend and sway even though there's hardly any breeze.

At the side of the track are rows of square wooden beehives, painted pale blue, cream and pink. Many of them are laid on a kind of wooden track to keep them off the ground. There are rocks on the tops of most of them, presumably to stop the lids blowing away. There don't seem to be bees in any of them.

On the left hand side of the path, the land drops away steeply towards the valley floor.

The trees are so thick that very little light gets through. A fig tree at the side of the road smells delicious in the heat.

About ten minutes from the house, Dad discovers a narrow path that leads off from the dirt road. We follow it and after a few hundred metres we reach a barrier made of brushwood. We can hear running water.

Dad says, "We've never let anything like this stop us, and

we're not about to start now." He climbs over the brushwood; Mum and I follow him.

We are in an olive orchard. The trees are old, battered and absolutely still in the shelter of the forest. They are loaded with tiny pale green pellets which will ripen in time to be harvested in the autumn. There are also a few orange trees but no one has bothered to pick the fruit and most of it has fallen. The oranges glow in the dust like jewels. Many of them have started to rot but Dad picks up a couple of good ones in case, he says, he has to endure another evening of 'granny drinks'.

The running water we could hear turns out to be a small spring that trickles through the middle of the orchard. Dad says that it's surprising that it's still running at this time of year.

"I'd have thought it would have dried up by now. That must be why the orchard is here and why someone thinks it's worth trying to keep people out."

We wander through the trees, taking care not to stumble on the loose rocks that cover the ground.

At the edge of the orchard we find the remains of what must have been a tiny village of five or six small houses, not much bigger than garden sheds really.

The walls are built of stone and are only three or four courses high, although in one house there's a perfect stone arch which must once have been a fireplace.

There's also an entire window frame, leaning against a wall. The glass is long gone, of course, and the wood has been bleached the palest grey in the sun, although there are still a few traces of brown paint.

Rocks and bits of timber are scattered everywhere. Broken

pantiles. Thistles, brambles and poppies are growing through the stones and have taken over most of the walls. A couple of small brown lizards scuttle for cover.

You can practically feel the people who lived here, however long ago it was. It wouldn't be surprising if a face appeared at the old broken window and asked us what the hell we think we're doing.

Dad says, "This must have been a pretty tough place to live. The mosquitoes would have been terrible, and you'd probably have to have had cloven hoofs to move about on such a steep slope. Presumably, the people cleared out of here pretty sharpish as soon as they got the chance. I wonder when that was. Could have been twenty years ago or a hundred, for all I know. Probably emigrated or moved to the coast to start a hotel. In search of an easier life. I wonder why no one's bothered to develop this place. Clear a few of those trees and the view would be spectacular."

Mum says that it would be a tragedy to cut down any of these trees. That they could be a thousand years old.

We wander about for another few minutes but it's starting to get really hot.

Mum says, "Let's go back to the villa for a drink."

She says, "There's something sad about this place. I don't just mean because of the old houses. It feels like we're trespassing; it feels like we're disturbing something."

And I know exactly what she means. This is a place of secrets. Like Mum, I can feel them, sense them in the air, even if it's impossible to say what they are.

Quail kebabs

This afternoon I drove us to the local beach; a bit disappointing really.

Finding it was hard enough. We had to follow this ridiculously steep dirt track down to the village—haven't they ever heard of tarmac? One of the turns was totally blind—just by a café, outside which were a load of old geezers drinking *ayran* (good luck to them) and playing backgammon. Then under the main road to a little town by the sea. Down the main street, then turn left at the inevitable Ataturk Square with the inevitable statue of the man himself and nothing much happening. You then drive through forest for a while (with no idea whether or not you are going in the right direction and no signs to guide you) and then get into a one-way system on a narrow coastal road that clings to the rocks.

After a few more kilometres, we came across loads of cars parked all over the place, making it almost impossible to drive past. So, we stopped. There's a gate and a steep path that leads down through some more trees to a café. People were picnicking at rough tables and benches in the trees.

There's a spring running through the rocks which ends in a little waterfall which tumbles into a pool just to the side of the café. Kids were jumping in and splashing about and squealing. There were a few small fish in the water. Presumably terrified by all the jumping and splashing, but unable to get out.

By the bogs an old man was sitting on his own, smoking a cigarette and with a cardboard box on his knees. There was a peeping noise coming from inside it. Of course, Maggie had to stop and bid the old bugger good afternoon and gesture that she wanted to know what was in the box. He opened it. Inside were about two dozen tiny chicks. They might have been quails. Maggie did a pantomime act the purpose of which was to ask him if they were rearing these tiny scraps of life so that they would lay eggs for the café. She even tucked her hands under her armpits and moved her elbows up and down. Clucked. The old guy stared at her in astonishment for a full minute, not saying anything. Then understanding dawned. He smiled a broken toothed smile at her and slowly drew his finger across his throat. Maggie looked shocked as I think he wanted her to. He laughed. These poor little sods were shortly for the cooking pot. Or maybe they were destined to end up on kebab sticks, little tiny frazzled morsels. Hardly a crunch between them.

A kid of about fifteen rented us sunbeds. They seemed remarkably cheap until we saw them. They were fine in themselves it's just that they were packed in so tightly together with everyone else's. The beach is pretty small and I guess they were maximizing the amount of business they could do. Trouble was that there wasn't room to put your bags down between the beds because it wasn't clear who the strips of space belonged to. To one side of us was a Turkish family—parents and three kids under ten—on the other side was a young couple in their twenties. Somewhere, not far away, someone was treating the entire beach to some Turkish disco music. The only thing I could hear in its favour is that it is marginally better than French disco music. And I mean *marginally*.

The bay is small and \/-shaped and looks due south. To the east, a few kilometres away, you can see the harbour wall of the small seaside town that we had just driven through. The sea flows swiftly between the beach and a little island about a kilometre away, and beyond that is a finger of land jutting out into the sea. It's covered with trees and looks startlingly green against the blue of the sea and sky. An occasional yacht or small fishing boat passed between us and the island.

The beach is pebbly and shelves slowly downwards. The water is crystal clear. It was also full of families swimming, some of the women in bikinis and swimsuits, some in something more like an Edwardian bathing dress—all sleeves and legs— and some in what seem to be their normal everyday clothes. They looked picturesque enough but it can't be much fun swimming with the weight of all those clothes hanging around you.

One group of women stepped fully clothed into the water, swam out about fifty metres and bobbed up and down chatting for at least an hour. From the tone of their laughter, I guessed they were talking about their husbands.

The water was warm enough in the shallows but as I swam further out it got much colder. And then I suddenly hit an icy cold patch that made my bones go numb. I think this must be where the stream near the café discharges into the bay. Then it was warmer again for a moment, and then bone-achingly cold again. It was like swimming through something with stripes.

I lay on my back and looked up at the sky. That way, I

couldn't hear the bobbing women yakking or the pop-up disco. I felt what I always feel in the water: bliss. Everything else just melts away. I'm not conscious of thinking anything much. Just of the water holding me up and the sunlight pouring all over me.

Maybe it's a kind of reverse evolution; a deep rooted desire to return to the water from which we emerged. Maybe it's something to do with the human body being two thirds water. But maybe it's much simpler than that. Maybe it's just that it feels brilliant.

I wish Maggie could share the experience with me. But she says that she never really feels comfortable in the sea. She swims well enough, but doesn't seem able to relax. Spends the time thinking about how to keep her neck straight and her head up. Thinks too much about breathing, which is, I suppose, fair enough.

Anyway, after the swim, I went for a walk. When you round the point of this tiny bay, a beach of white stones and pebbles opens up in front of you. It's obviously marshy here because reeds as tall as I am come right down to the shoreline. Loads of small black and white birds were skimming over the reeds.

A number of families were camped on the beach (presumably they resented paying the 15TL necessary to use the café's facilities). Somehow they'd managed to get cars down here and had loads of kit: barbecue sets, chairs, blankets and masses of food and drink—salads, melons, heaps of oranges, huge piles of flatbread, gallons of Coke and Fanta.

In some of these groups, elderly relatives were holding court from what looked like (and probably were) indoor armchairs. I saw a couple of guys open the back of a transit van. Inside was a large brown padded chair with wooden legs and on it was a tiny old lady—nothing more really than a collection of wrinkles held together by her clothes—who must have been at least a hundred. Each bloke grabbed one arm of the chair and carried great-great-granny onto the beach, her little legs flapping in space.

A different couple of guys were fishing, but I didn't see anyone catch anything. Inevitably, someone else was playing Turkish disco music, but no one seemed to be objecting. Maybe they even liked it.

In many ways it was an idyllic scene; the only problem was the rubbish: plastic bags, broken glass, millions of cigarette butts, bog paper, disposable nappies, deflated footballs, unexplained items of clothing, orange bailer twine, drink cans. It was everywhere. But the picnickers seemed hardly more aware of it than they were of the music. Certainly, they didn't seem to have made any attempt to clear up around them. Just sat in and, I guess in some cases, made their own contributions to the mountain of crap that had once been a beautiful beach.

Meanwhile, the sea lapped back and forth indifferently.

CLICK

The full moon has emerged above the trees and is washing the road and the trees behind the villa and the walls of the ruined houses with pale light.

The tops of the pines shiver gently, almost imperceptibly.

But the moonlight can scarcely penetrate the thickest parts of the forest where every branch is hung with lichen and every trunk trussed with ivy. Where every patch of ground is carpeted with brambles.

In the darkest part of the wood a female boreal owl is making her disapproval felt. She's flapping her wings angrily and clicking her beak in frustration. Click. Click. Click.

It's time for her children to leave.

She turns her white disc of a face away from them and clicks her yellow beak,

Click. Click. Click. CLICK.

They are almost eight weeks old and fledged. She's done her bit and now it's time for them to find their own hunting grounds. Her decision is final. She will not feed them any longer. It's not a question of shortage of food. This is a time of plenty. It's just that she no longer has the energy for it.

Besides, her children have ceased to exist for her. A shutter has come down in her brain, excluding them, cutting them off from her forever.

The problem is that they have not yet accepted this. The three of them are perched on branches close to her and are calling for food.

Hiss. Hiss. Hiss.

They are still hoping for one last shrew or lizard or large spider. Still huddling together for comfort as the stars wheel round the night sky. Still roosting together during the days in the stifling hole of a hollow trunk.

Hiss. Hiss. Hiss.

Calling incessantly.

This will go on for some time. Until the fear of starvation will finally send them on their way.

Eventually, the mother will be left alone until it's time to mate again. Possibly with this year's male; more probably with another or others.

And then everything will begin again.

Click. Click. CLICK. CLICK.

The Marble City of Eternal Love and Gladiators

The road corkscrews up the side of a thousand metre cliff, turning back on itself and then back again and again, as your ears pop.

The valley floor seems to be directly under the car and every time you look down it makes your stomach turn over.

We're on a trip to visit an ancient city called Stratonikeia.

Mum says that it's not in most guidebooks, that most people have never heard of it, and that it was known as the 'Marble City of Eternal Love and Gladiators'. The two things don't seem to have much to do with each other.

Dad says that if the gladiators were struck with eternal love for each other they probably weren't very good gladiators, which might be why no one's ever heard of 'Stratoni-whatever-its-name-is'

Mum says it will be very 'improving'.

Dad says that maybe the people of 'Stratoni-doo-dah' went to see gladiators in the afternoon and got down to a bit of eternal love in the evenings. So perhaps it wasn't the gladiators who were struck with eternal love after all.

Mum puts her fingers in her ears and says, "Whatever. La la la. We're going."

At the side of the road, there are lots of stalls selling large china donkeys, camels and sheep. No one seems to be buying anything. There are also stalls with huge heaps of oranges, one of which has a sign saying 'Vitamin C Stop'. No one seems to be stopping.

It looks like some of the people trying to sell stuff spend the whole summer up here. They have camper vans and tents and barbecues set up. In a couple of places, the vans are parked on the *outside* of the crash barrier and are hanging over a terrifying sheer drop. You certainly wouldn't want to get out of bed on the wrong side if you lived there.

Most of the cars and lorries on the road are new and powerful, but a few are old and falling to bits, loaded with watermelons or goats, only doing about ten kilometres an hour and puffing out clouds of exhaust fumes. No one seems to mind that they don't pull over to allow cars behind to pass.

No one, that is, apart from Dad: "I don't suppose anyone here's ever considered looking in a mirror... It's a privilege to breathe their exhaust fumes." And so on.

Mountains march off into the distance as far as the eye can see. Some of them are bald on top, some just thinning. Sometimes we catch a glimpse of blue—the sea sparkling way, way below us.

An hour ago, there wasn't a cloud in the sky, but now they seem to be piling up from every direction, towering thousands and thousands of metres in the air, reaching across almost from one horizon to the other.

After about twenty minutes the ground levels out. We've reached the top. We pass through villages which have been sliced in half by the road. Neighbours who used to be able to drop in on one another now have to cross a four-lane motorway every time they want to borrow a cup of sugar.

The sky is thick with clouds.

We stop for a while at a street market. There are stalls selling oranges, melons, grapefruit, lemons, potatoes, tomatoes, cucumbers, lettuces, olives, aubergines, onions, courgettes, garlic, mushrooms, artichokes, cherries, strawberries, peppers, green beans, beetroots, apricots. And those are just the things I can identify. Other stalls have honey or yoghurt or cheese or nuts. In one corner, they're selling T shirts and trainers and bedspreads and Turkish women's trousers and headphones. As soon as they realize that we're from England, the guys selling things practise their English on us, saying things like: 'genuine fakes', 'Manchester United' and 'at these prices I'm robbing myself'. One of them offers Mum a 'genuine' Rolex watch— 'with finest movement'—for 50TL.

It's still incredibly hot and steamy and the sky is black.

Dad asks if we're still headed for 'Stratoni-thingummy'. Mum says that it's only about another ten kilometres.

The road takes us up and over another range of ear-popping mountains. There are more and more mountains as far as the eye can see.

Dad says, "I don't know about ten kilometres. We must have been driving for half an hour. I guess it's too much to expect there to be a sign."

Mum says, "Look, that must be a mirage up ahead, it looks like water."

What appears to be a stream in the middle of the road is flowing down the hill towards us. And what's more, it doesn't disappear as we travel towards it. It's for real.

To begin with it's hardly more than a trickle but it gradually widens to fill the whole road to a depth of about ten centimetres

Suddenly, it's raining so hard that Dad can hardly see.

"Where are the bloody headlights on this thing?"

The rain is so heavy that it blots out the light and makes a scary noise on the roof of the car. The rest of the traffic has slowed to a crawl.

Dad says, "If it gets any heavier we'll be floating to Stratoni-oojah. I'd stop but I haven't a clue whether or not I'm allowed to and I don't want one of those old bangers full of watermelons or goats ploughing into the back of us."

After a few minutes the rain does ease a bit and we can see a little more of the road. Water is pouring down the rocks at the side and then spilling straight off the edge.

Suddenly, Mum says, "I think I just saw a sign for Stratonikeia."

"Where?"

"About fifty metres back."

"Brilliant. These signs are so helpful. And I can't turn round because this is still dual carriageway."

In fact we have to drive for about another five minutes before we can turn, then we have to drive a few more kilometres past the sign before we can turn again and approach Stratonikeia from the correct direction.

Dad drives slowly along a dirt track with huge puddles in it. There are orchards on either side of the track and prickly pears growing on the verges. There are no other cars.

After a few hundred metres we come to a bend in the track. Someone has hung a rope across it from one tree to another.

Someone else has untied one end and the rope's now lying on the ground. Dad says that we might as well go on.

Eventually we come to a short, steep hill. Dad is only moving slowly but as soon as we get onto the slope, the car starts to slide from side to side. Fishtailing. Dad's knuckles go white on the steering wheel and I can see that Mum is very tense.

"Jesus. I can only just control this thing."

On one side of the slope is a deep ditch, on the other, the land drops away into the orchards.

After about thirty seconds of this, the ground levels out again. On our right is a chain link fence behind which we can see the stone foundations of some buildings and the lower parts of some columns. We've finally arrived at the City of Eternal Love and Gladiators. The only problem is that it's clearly shut. There's no one around. No gladiators and no one expressing their eternal love for anyone else.

On our left is a small ticket booth, inside which is a bloke waving to us. Dad gets out and wades through the puddles to the booth.

We can see him waving his arms and we can see the bloke inside the booth waving his arms back.

After a bit more of this, Dad comes back, his sandals full of mud, and says, "Needless to say, he doesn't speak English. I asked him why the place is shut and how we get out of here but he didn't have a clue what I was on about. And when he did speak, I didn't have a clue what he was on about. He kept pointing at the sky and shaking his head. So, I guess he's saying that it's closed because of the rain. Probably for the first time in two thousand years. Problem is that now we're here, we've got to find our way out again."

The man is the booth is waving again. He steps out and wades through the puddles to the car.

Dad winds down the window and the bloke hands him a bottle of water. He shrugs and looks helpless. Then he wades through the puddles back to his booth.

Then, before Mum and I realize what he's going to do, Dad turns the car round, guns the engine and heads straight for the slope.

Mum just has time to say, "Are you sure about this?" before we hit the slope. The engine is racing and the car is sliding all over the place. Mud is coating the windshield.

Dad yells, "Come on car."

The windscreen wipers are trying and failing to clear the mud. The engine is roaring. The tyres are spinning. The back of the car is behaving in a way that seems to have nothing to do with the way the front of the car is behaving.

And then, quite suddenly, we're up, back onto the shingle track. We've made it.

Mum says, "My hero."

Dad says, "It was nothing. But I'll tell you what: I'm never coming back to Stratoni-whosit. Never, ever. No matter how long I live. No matter how much you beg."

We stop in a lay-by.

It's started to rain heavily again but Dad says he needs to check that there's no damage to the car.

He gets out and walks round it in the lashing rain.

And then he starts to laugh, which he does for quite a long

time, while Mum and I sit in the car and look at him.

When he gets back in, Mum asks what was so funny?

"Oh, nothing."

As we start the drive back to the villa, the weather lifts, the clouds disappear and the sun comes out again.

Guests

At the wedding party, Meric, who has the misfortune to be married to the appalling Serkan, whose eyes look in different directions, whispered a story about one of her guests. She has a job cleaning at the horrible orange villa on the edge of the village that is owned by the stock broker from Ankara. It must have cost a fortune and they only use it a couple of weeks a year. For most of the summer, they lend it to friends and family or rent it to paying guests. In winter, it stands empty. Anyway, on this particular morning, Meric was mopping the kitchen floor and minding her own business while the family—a very fat man, his glamorous wife and two children— were playing by the pool. She realized that the man had come into the room and was staring at her. Suddenly, he pulled his (tiny) swimming trunks down and looked at her as if he was expecting something, although she wasn't sure what. A gasp of admiration? A howl of outrage? A whimper of terror? She didn't feel able to do any of these things. She said that he might be the meanest man alive and have eyes that look round corners and not have anything resembling passion in his emotional makeup, but compared with this man with his stomach folds and teeny manhood, even Serkan was a real stud, a stallion. She said that she wanted to laugh but, at the same time, was worried that his wife would come into the room and think that she had somehow encouraged such behaviour. And that would mean no tip at the end of the week. She couldn't leave the room because he was blocking the doorway, so she did the only thing possible: said nothing and carried on with her mopping, working her way round him as he stood there with his trunks round his ankles. At one point he had to lift his left foot so that the mop could pass under it and clean the spot on which he was standing. Eventually he pulled his trunks up and left the room.

We were all shocked but we also thought it was hilarious. We laughed so much that the wedding singer looked offended and sang even louder and people started shushing us.

But Meric's story opened the flood gates. Many of the women round our table are cleaners and housekeepers and cooks in villas and suddenly they all wanted to tell their stories. Stories of things found in the shower that belonged in the lavatory, of used condoms in unmade beds, of insolent teenagers, of wedding rings in the garbage, of extreme drunkenness and nudity, of third degree sunburn, of inexplicable stains on the walls, of vomit in cupboards, of babysitting for appalling, psychopathic children, of an amputated toe in a pool.

Cemile said that she once found an entire set of false teeth on the mantelpiece of the house she was cleaning. The guests had left for the airport many hours before and would clearly not be coming back for them. She said they gave her quite a fright because they were grinning so widely that they reminded her of a mad person. She couldn't understand how anyone could forget something so important. At what point would they discover that they were missing and what would they then do? Cemile said that because she didn't know what to do with them, she wrapped them in a piece of cloth and put them in a drawer. She had meant to ask her employer what he thought would be the best thing. But she forgot all about it until the next guests arrived and found the teeth while they were searching for candles during a power cut. They were not amused and complained to the owner who had words with her. In the end she took them home with her and put them in the drawer of her kitchen table. Apparently, her grandchildren often ask if they can play with them. Nothing has ever been heard from the original owners.

Burcak once walked into what she thought was an empty bedroom only to discover the guests having sex on the floor in what she said looked like a very uncomfortable position. She was so startled that she screamed. The woman on the floor instantly disentangled herself from the uncomfortable position (Burcak said that she had time to be impressed by her obvious gymnastic ability) and dived onto the bed and under the covers, from where Burcak could hear her laughing. The man on the floor was not so agile and it took him a moment of two to get to his feet, at which point he jumped into the wardrobe, pulling the door shut behind him. She could hear all the metal coat hangers clattering around in there while he shouted at her to get out. Burcak said that as she shut the door behind her she could still hear the woman in the bed laughing fit to bust. Her tip that week was double what she normally expects.

Melek said that from what she has seen of such people it wouldn't have surprised her if they had invited Burcak to join them on the floor. Maybe her tip then would have been four times normal. For a moment there was a sharp, scandalized intake of breath around the table and then we all fell about laughing. The wedding singer looked even more annoyed. Maybe he was worried that we were having a better time than the people listening to his singing. Which, to tell the truth, we were.

Nesrin, who speaks quite good English, told how she had once been asked to babysit for some people who were on holiday from London. She arrived expecting to look after a child or children and so was astonished to find that they wanted her to look after a very old lady. She was the husband's mother and they had felt that they couldn't leave her back in England. The old lady was clearly in the later stages of dementia but the husband and wife assured Nesrin that she was placid and wouldn't cause any difficulty and that they would only be at the restaurant two hours max. Promise. Nesrin reluctantly agreed only after they had reluctantly given her the number of the husband's mobile in case of emergencies. Things started well but soon started to go wrong. Nesrin and the old lady settled down to watch TV. First they watched the international news which was obviously making the old lady unhappy. So Nesrin flicked through the channels until she found an old soap that the old lady seemed to recognize. Nesrin found it hard to follow even though it had Turkish subtitles and the next thing she knew was that she was waking up out of a deep sleep and the old lady wasn't there any longer. Where she had been sitting was a neat pile of her clothes. In a panic, she searched the villa but there was no sign of the old lady. This was truly awful. She went into the garden and there she was as naked as the day she was born, lying in a flower bed looking at the stars. Of course, Nesrin tried to persuade her to get up and come inside. But she wouldn't. So then she tried ringing the husband on his mobile but he didn't pick up. In the end, she put her hands under the old lady's armpits and hauled her to her feet and half carried, half led her indoors. By this time, the old lady had started singing in a quavery voice and seemed to be enjoying herself.

Nesrin looked up and just at that moment a shooting star flashed across the sky. She said that seeing it made her feel even more hopeless and alone and out of her depth. Anyway, the old lady was by now very excited and very reluctant to put her clothes on again. It took a couple of hours cajoling and persuading to get her into her nightie and tucked up in bed. Five hours after they had left, the husband and wife retuned from the restaurant, so drunk that they could barely stand. Because she had nearly lost the old lady, Nesrin didn't think she could complain, couldn't tell them that this had been one of the worst, most frightening nights of her life. The husband fished a few notes out of his pocket and handed them to her, barely bothering to say thank you. It wasn't until she was back in her own house that Nesrin realized that she had only been paid for four hours and that there was no tip.

On and on the stories went. I don't know what these people think of us, but I often wonder if they ever think how peculiar their lives seem to us.

The garden

After all that excitement yesterday, Mum and Dad have decided that we'll be spending today by the pool. Dad says that he feels like he needs a holiday, having driven through a 'typhoon' and negotiated an 'avalanche'.

The pool's only about twenty metres from the front door but it seems we have to take a huge amount of stuff with us—sun cream, books, bottles of water, towels, reading glasses, binoculars, hats, a guidebook, a bag of crisps—all of which completely fills two beach bags. It actually *is* like going on holiday all over again. So, Dad ought to be pleased.

He and Mum cover themselves in sun cream, lie on the sunbeds and are immediately absorbed in their books.

His is about an ex-military policeman who can't find love and instead manages to have a different adventure in every single US state, including Wyoming.

Hers is about a secret that has been passed through the generations of an Australian family. A secret that has the power to tear families apart.

They look like they going to be here for some time.

I lie with them for a while, but I've never been than keen on sunbathing and I don't have anything that I want to read. So, I look at the sky for a bit, and then I say that I'm going for a walk. Mum and Dad are too absorbed in their books about violence and secrets to take much notice. I say that I'll be back in time for lunch.

Instead of turning left on the track above the house as we did the other morning, I turn right. The track leads down past the Basaks' house where chickens are scratching around in the flowerbeds. I pass a couple of new villas on the side of the hill. They have white walls and orange roofs and there are masses of scarlet flowers growing up them. There's obviously no one at home. It's very hot and the cicadas are shrieking their heads off. I do what I can to walk in the shade.

After a sharp S-bend, the track passes into some thick trees. It's cooler in here but not much. A lizard shoots out from under my feet. I have no idea where the track leads, but I keep walking. Always downwards.

After a while, I come across a cemetery in the forest. This is not what I was expecting. It's very peaceful here with marble gravestones scattered between the trees. There's a distant view of the sea. For a minute, I wonder who all these people were and what their lives were like. But it makes my head hurt. So I stop wondering.

I follow the track still further downwards, passing a couple of goats grazing on the edge of a field. Eventually, I come to the outskirts of a small village. Most of the houses are built of wood and stone and are only one storey high. Their doors and shutters are painted pale blue. There are a couple of new villas with satellite dishes and high walls around them. They don't really seem to belong.

I come to the village square which has an enormous tree that must be hundreds of years old and (just for a change) a statue of

Ataturk. A number of old men are smoking on a bench under the tree and one of them looks up as I pass. But I'm too shy to approach them. The others ignore me.

One of the cottages near the square has an enormous nest on its chimney stack. In it there are two huge scruffy birds with black and white wings and long red beaks. I think they must be chicks even though they're so big. Otherwise, why would they be here?

The nest is a real mess; twigs all over the place and bits of cardboard and plastic in it. It doesn't smell too good either; a kind of bitter, stale smell. The chicks must be frying in the sun, baking their little birdie brains. There's a thick layer of bird shit on the roof.

While I'm watching, there's a noise in the sky and one of the parent birds swoops in with an eel or a snake wriggling in its beak. It passes this to one of the chicks which somehow manages to swallow it whole. The parent bird takes off again, flying in ever larger circles to gain height, like someone climbing a spiral staircase.

An old man passes on a tractor. I smile and half wave at him but he doesn't take any notice.

I'm really hot and thirsty and I know I've got to climb back up the hill. But just five minutes more.

We must have driven past it yesterday and I almost walk past it now without noticing. In a stretch of old wall at the side of the road is a broken, arched wooden double door, with huge rusted metal hinges. The left hand side is hanging at a weird angle. The right hand side is still in the closed position. An overgrown climbing rose has smothered the wall in bright red flowers.

There's a stone step about fifty centimetres high and it's as if the thistles and nettles on the threshold are trying to keep people out.

But as Dad says, we've never let anything like that stop us. I push through the hanging door and, even though I'm wearing shorts, I don't get stung.

I'm in what obviously used to be a garden. The grass is burnt to a pale honey colour by the sun. There are great spikes of cream and blue and scarlet flowers everywhere, with millions of bees constantly bumping in to them. As I move through them, I can see where the flower beds used to be. The walls are covered with climbing plants and ivy. There are orange and lemon trees with most of the fruit on the ground. Old broken tools— spades, rakes, hoes, a sieve—are scattered around. The crickets are sawing away.

It's very weird. Although I've never been here before, it feels familiar. It's like a place I've seen in a dream.

In one corner of the plot is a pile of stone. I clear away the plants around it and realize that what I'm looking at is the remains of a small fountain. There's a kind of basin in the shape of a shell.

Nearby are two trees—one shorter than the other—which twist and turn and look like they are corkscrewing themselves out of the ground and aiming for the sky. They look like flames. Like ghosts. Like fountains. They are beautiful and elegant and out of the ordinary and they know it. These are trees with a strong personality.

I sit in the long grass and watch a column of ants marking a trail in the dust. There are butterflies everywhere and small black and white birds with swept back wings swing and twitch around the place. Crickets leap about on springs. The heat beats down. I feel completely happy.

At this moment, if I knew I could never leave this place, I don't think I'd mind.

Something is moving in the grass—a mouse, a frog, a snake?—but I can't see it. I have this sense I'm being watched. That I'm not alone. But, of course, there's no one here apart from me. Maybe what I'm feeling is the presence of the people who used to live here.

I sit in the shade of the trees and feel so sleepy that I wonder if I'm ever going to be able to get up again and head back to the villa.

Ghost children

When Seyhan goes away, I always put on this act about how distraught I am, how I won't know what to do with myself, how I will starve without her cooking, and how I will cry myself to sleep at night. And, of course, everyone laughs and sympathises.

What they don't know is that I am telling the truth, that this is what I really feel. That I'm hiding in plain sight. That my hammed up despair conceals an unbearable reality.

The truth is that the house feels empty without her and my life seems empty without her. The truth is that I am *nothing* without her. That when she's not here, I can't sleep and wander round the house like a ghost. My only consolation is my garden. Which is why Urfuz often finds me already working in it when he arrives at dawn to clean the pool. But he is far too discrete to comment on this fact; just waves and gets on with his work. If he is surprised, he doesn't show it. But I think it would take a lot to surprise Urfuz and a lot more to persuade him to show it. Expressiveness is not really his thing, except when we killed that snake last year. He got excited enough for both of us then.

Every few months, Seyhan goes to visit her mother who is in a nursing home in Ankara. She has done this throughout our marriage. In the early years, when her mother was still living in her own home, Seyhan used to stay with her there. And I have learned to accept it. I drive her to the airport and continue to crack jokes. I never reveal that I have been dreading this moment since she made the booking. And, of course, she must never know this. It would be too heavy a burden for her to bear.

At least this time I've been spared all those weeks of anticipation. The call came last night; her mother has heart failure, could she come at once?

The awful truth is that, in secret, part of me hopes that her mother will die, and that Seyhan will not have to go to Ankara again. What kind of man must I be to think that? No kind of man that I could approve of. Certainly not the kind of man that Seyhan would knowingly have married.

I remember the first time I saw her. She was in a restaurant having coffee with a cousin of mine. She had just returned from America—where she had been on a university scholarship—and dressed differently from any of the other (very few) women I knew. She was not exactly beautiful, but she seemed cool and remote and glamorous.

I was shy but I forced myself to go across to the table. My cousin did not look pleased. I sometimes think how different my life would have been if I hadn't had that moment's courage.

She told me that her ambition was to be a teacher of Greek and Latin in a high school, to bring Homer and Virgil to Turkey's children; that the next step was to complete her teaching qualification. She said that she was staying with her aunt's family nearby; that her home was in Ankara. By the way she was looking at me, I could tell that she thought I was a fool, a bumpkin, a hick who had never travelled further from home than to the neighbouring province.

I didn't know how to behave: the more I talked, the clearer it would become that I was an idiot; but the less I talked, the more likely she was to think of me as a total dullard.

However, when she left—after insisting on paying for her coffee in spite of my cousin's florid protestations and mine—I knew exactly what I had to do. I demanded that my cousin give me her address. He was very disinclined but I insisted and he gave in.

I wrote to her—I must have drafted that letter a hundred times—asking if she would consider coming for a walk with me one evening. To my astonishment, she replied straight away, saying that she would like it very much. But that first of all it would be necessary for me to meet her aunt and would I like to come to her aunt's house the following Saturday at five for çay and pastries?

That first time, we walked down through the trees to the beach. It was one of those evenings when the sea and the sky merged like the inside of a hinged shell. It was so quiet and still that I thought my heart might break. I was inexpressibly happy. I was immensely sad. If the sea could have swallowed us up together that evening, I would have considered my life fulfilled. Of course, I was not so stupid as to tell her any of this.

We talked about our childhood—hers in Ankara, mine in Kinzmik—our educations, our friends and families. I am an only child and my father, an accountant, had been dead for years; she is one of five (four brothers) and her father had been a successful doctor, but he too had died young leaving her mother to raise her family on little money.

We were both, I think, careful not to talk about the future.

But I already knew what mine would be and had started to make plans. But again, I did not make the mistake of revealing any of this to her.

Nothing was said, but when I delivered her back into her aunt's care, I knew that in some way I could not explain things had moved forward and that my path in life was now irreversible. Besides, I could tell that her aunt—a regal woman, as tall as a man, dressed in a velvet robe and turban—approved of me, even though I only came up to her shoulder.

As a newly qualified lawyer, I knew that my future would require me to travel. Somehow, I had to persuade Seyhan that her future was bound up with mine and that she too would have to uproot herself. The fact that she had spent that year in America and left her parental home gave me great hope. I knew already that she would never give up on the idea of teaching, that she would only find total happiness in bringing *The Odyssey* and Caesar's *Gallic Wars* to generations of bored, hormonal schoolkids. But at least she would be able to find work wherever my career took me.

And if the worst came to the worst and she was unwilling for whatever reason to move, well, then I would have to abandon my career and find work locally, any kind of work. It would be a small price to pay.

And, of course, we never had any children. I always told Seyhan that I could quite literally not conceive of having them. I made it sound like a political decision, like I couldn't bear to bring a kid into a world as messed up as this. And part of me does believe that. But the real reason was that I could not bear to share her with anyone, could not bear to lose her to a son or daughter. She agreed, reluctantly. I think she felt that there was no point in trying to persuade me, because the need for persuasion simply proved my unfitness for fatherhood.

I think the decision was made a little easier for her because she has been able to express her nurturing instincts in her relationships with her pupils. She was always the first to volunteer for school trips, always inviting favoured pupils home for lunch and supper.

But in some ways our marriage has been haunted. Our house is inhabited by the children we never had. They crowd in everywhere. They have prevented us from ever entirely relaxing into our marriage, ever entirely taking it for granted. You can't walk from one room to another without bumping into them.

Seyhan and I have never spoken of them, but we both know they are there. Our house echoes with unanswered questions that have never been asked.

Selfies

This afternoon we drove to the local seaside town to do some shopping in a tiny supermarket. But it was worth it because Dad finally got his hands on some tonic even though it was only the supermarket's own brand and he had a good moan about the prices.

Mum seemed to enjoy herself and Dad had almost to drag her away from the woman at the till just before, as he said, she started to ask her about her husband and children and what school they went to.

We wandered around the town for a while. Apparently it's really popular with Turkish tourists and there has been loads of building going on in the last few years. Hotels, pensions and guest houses are appearing everywhere, along with restaurants and souvenir and carpet shops.

The houses in a couple of the streets are obviously much older with complicated wooden balconies. The walls are painted a lemony yellow.

At the point where the road enters the town there's a large stone building like a giant igloo with a perfectly smooth domed roof.

Dad stopped the car and we all got out to take a look. There's an inscription carved into a stone above the door and a hand-painted sign giving an English translation.

Apparently, it's a water cistern which was given to the people of the town by a man who described himself as a 'customs officer and a tax collector', in memory of his 'much loved' dead wife, 'the adornment of his home'. It looks hundreds of years old but in fact was only built in the 1840s. The tax collector and his wife had been married for thirty eight years and she had 'bored him' seven children. According to the inscription, she was also famous throughout the neighbourhood for her hospitality and her charitable works.

The building was used to collect rainwater; not for drinking but for local people's gardens and animals. I suppose they must have been grateful. Who knows?

After shopping, we went to a café for a drink. You go through a small courtyard in which there is a fountain and a palm tree and come out onto a wooden platform built onto one bank of a fast flowing, shallow river. The platform sticks out three or four metres, which meant that the water passed directly under where we were sitting. It was incredibly clear and we could see the weed being tugged around by the current.

Nearby, boys a bit younger than me were swimming. Two geese and a lot of chicks swept past us. Somehow the chicks managed to turn and paddle upstream, their legs working furiously.

On the other side of the river is a reed bed; the reeds are taller than me. Hundreds of electric blue dragonflies zigzagged up and down while swallows dipped down to drink or clung on to one of the reeds. I don't suppose a swallow weighs much, but even so the reeds bent under them. Just before they were tipped into the water, they were off—hunting for more insects or just having a good time, and the reeds sprang up straight again.

As we walked down towards the town, the river widened, slowed and deepened. We passed a couple more cafés, some tea stalls and a guy selling necklaces.

We came to a green metal bridge. A gang of guys were jumping off the bridge while their mates filmed them from the bank on their mobile phones. Once in the water, the current swept them about fifty metres downstream before they could swim to the bank. A bloke on the deck of a moored yacht was hauling them out of the water.

One guy was trying to take a selfie in mid-air. Unlike the others who just dropped over the side of the bridge, he stood on the railing and then jumped as high and as far as he could with his arms out. He did a sort of half turn and clicked his phone in front of his face, smiling madly before hitting the water. As soon as the bloke on the yacht had yanked him out, he checked his screen but he obviously wasn't satisfied with the results because he kept doing it again and again.

One guy tried to dive rather than jump but his foot slipped at the last moment and he did a horrendous belly-flop. When he came to the surface you could tell that he was trying not to show how much it hurt. His mates howled with laughter and took photographs of him.

After the bridge, the river opened up into a harbour with high walls. Dozens of yachts were moored there along with a floating café selling chicken nuggets.

Right next to the harbour is the public beach. Turkish disco music was blaring from huge speakers. Dad pulled a face. There were millions of people. The sunbeds were packed in so tightly that no one was more than a few centimetres from his or her neighbour.

This was definitely not Mum and Dad's sort of place, so I don't think we'll be going there again soon.

Three pirate ships, flying the skull and crossbones from their masts, appeared round the headland. Dad groaned. The music from them was so loud that you could feel it through your feet. All three crews were dressed as pirates: scarves round their heads, fake beards, eye patches and striped T shirts, ridiculous plastic cutlasses tucked into their belts.

The boats tied up at the harbour wall and the music stopped. The passengers got off—hundreds and hundreds of them; far more than you could believe would ever have fitted on board. Not really looking at anything, they walked straight to a convoy of waiting coaches and climbed in. The convoy then disappeared with a lot of honking of horns and clouds of diesel fumes.

Very definitely not Mum and Dad's sort of place.

Hot news: tonight, back at the villa, Dad made himself a gin and tonic, just as he likes it—more gin than tonic. He added a slice of lemon and looked into his glass for a while. It was as if he could see something in it that no one else could. The expression on his face was that of a man helplessly in love. Then he sipped his drink, closed his eyes, shook his shoulders and groaned—but in a good way.

Not a monumental bloke

If I died, would Steve put up a monument to me and, if so, what kind would it be? He doesn't strike me as a very monumental sort of bloke. And I know that if I asked him, he'd be bound to say something like a half-pipe for skateboarders or a horse trough or a public lavatory.

But, say what you like about that old tax collector, he didn't do things by halves. No park bench or municipal tree for him.

This was a very grand gesture, even if it was also a rather banal one. Had he planned it before she died, got an architect to draw up plans etc? In which case, he must have been a pretty weird man.

Or was he so overcome with sorrow that the only way he could express it was with a public building? In which case, he was even weirder.

His wife was around sixty when she died. Presumably of some illness or infection or maybe even of old age—I don't know how long people usually lived back then.

For some reason, I imagine her as tall and thin with white hair and a serene face.

I think she may have been a bit contemptuous of her husband; thought he was a bit of an idiot, prone to grand gestures, more likely to go over the top than to be understated.

I think she would have had her doubts about this monument

to her husband's grief. In all probability, the only monument she would have wanted was in the memories of her children

Whatever else, it must have cost a lot of money. But because, as I imagine her, she was analytical and a touch dry, cynical even, I'm sure she would have wondered how the people of the town would have interpreted such a gesture. Would they see a bereft man trying to express his sorrow, or would they see a man with an inevitably unpopular job attempting to buy popularity?

On the other hand, it *is* beautifully built, elegant even, and looks as though it's good for the next five hundred years. So I guess that however difficult to please she might have been, part of her would have thought that he could have done worse.

Ali

M um and Dad are sunbathing by the pool. Again. Boring.

They've finished their books and, because they couldn't be bothered to find something from the villa, they've swapped. So, now Dad is pursuing secrets through several generations of an Australian family. He keeps saying things like, "How likely is that?" and "For God's sake." Mum is breaking arms and putting bullets into the bad guys without a second thought and asking questions like, "Was that really necessary?" I don't think I can add much to this conversation so I decide to leave them to it. I want to visit the garden again.

The track above the villa is baking and the light is blinding. The hens are scrabbling about in Mr Basak's garden and the shadows of the trees are waving and dancing over the graves in the cemetery.

I can hear some strange, spooky music. It sounds like bells and the sound is coming towards me. There's a commotion in the undergrowth at the side of the track and a goat suddenly steps onto the path. It's close enough to touch. It looks at me in horror and stands stock still for a moment. Another one appears and almost bumps into it. Then another and another. The music is the noise of the bells round their necks. They all look at me in terror and circle around in a group at the side of the path getting as close to each other as possible, as if they don't know which way to go. They can't go back where they came from, because their path through the bushes is blocked by the goats that are still arriving at the track. I step to one side. Number one goat considers the situation for a moment. It looks at me and then at the track. It takes a step towards me and, when I don't move, breaks into a trot until it's got past me. Then it slows down again. The other goats now have a decision to make. One by one, they follow the first goat. Watching me nervously, trotting past me and then slowing to a walk. Not one of them looks back. Their bells tinkle and their hooves crunch on the stones. I can feel their disapproval from here.

As I get to the broken door in the wall, I can hear a noise coming from the garden, the noise of metal on stone. Someone else is in there. For a minute, I think I won't go in. I don't want to disturb whoever it is. But I'm really hot and the sun is making my head hurt. I remember how cool it was sitting under those beautiful trees. Maybe I'll chance it.

I step through the door and call out, "Hello." There's no answer and the noise of metal banging on stone continues. It sounds like someone's digging or hammering, but I can't see anyone.

I take a few paces inside the garden; everything is still apart from the clink, clink noise. I realize that whoever is making it is in the far corner, half hidden by the trees.

"Hello," I say again, more loudly. Nothing. I'm just about to say it for a third time, when a figure appears out of the long blonde grass. He must have been kneeling down and now stands up and stretches. He shades his eyes with his hand, looks straight

74

at me. He's wearing thick trousers, a dark waistcoat and a shirt without a collar. There's a trowel in his hand. He waves shyly. He looks as though I've surprised him. In fact, for a minute I'd say he looks scared of me. Maybe he's not meant to be here. I guess we're around the same age; maybe he's a year or so older.

"Hello," I say for the third time. And then, like an idiot, I ask, "Do you speak English?"

Of course he doesn't. But then, to my amazement he says, "Hello. Yes, I speak some English. But not so much as I should." He smiles.

He steps towards me and we shake hands awkwardly. He has one of those faces that you never forget; one of those faces that when you see it, you know what his mother and father look like. His father must be tall and skinny with a hooked nose; his mother is shorter, rounder, frecklier. Only that combination of DNA could possibly account for such a face. Or maybe his mother is the one with the hook nose, and his dad the freckles. But whichever way round it is, he looks like them and no one but them.

"Where did you learn to speak English?"

"I go to school in Istanbul. We learn English there."

"Isn't that a long way?"

"In term time my aunt looks after me in our apartment in Istanbul. My holidays, I spend here. With my father. He is working here."

"Is he staying in the village?"

"Not in the village. We have rented small cottage. It is near village. In the hills."

After that, we seem to run out of things to say for a minute.

I tell him that my name is Matt and he tells me that his is Ali.

"What are you doing?" I ask.

"I am digging. I am hoping to make archaeological find."

He tells me that there was an important Lycian settlement around her somewhere. It had a market place, a baths, a temple and a theatre, but has been forgotten. Over the centuries people have nicked all the building stone and now there is no record of exactly where the settlement was.

I say that I'd never heard of the Lycians until Mr Basak told Mum and Dad about them the other evening.

He says that they arrived in this part of Turkey maybe around three thousand years ago, and built cities at places like Xanthos and Tlos and Telmessos and Myra and Patara, as well as Dad's favourite: 'Stratoni-I'm-never-bleeding-going-there-again-in-my-life-keia').

Some of the stones from the vanished city can still be found in the walls of the houses and barns throughout the regions. A few of them have inscriptions carved on them.

For example, he says, one of the oldest houses in the village has an ancient Lycian carved stone over the doorway.

"The people who live there, do not know it but writing above their door says, '*This tomb is for Waziye and his mother.*' I wonder what they would think if they knew what the words mean."

He tells me that another house has a stone in the boundary wall which reads, "*Ebenne prnnawa me ti prnnawate eriminuha semuteh tideimi hrppi atli ehbi syeni ehbi.*"

When he speaks these words, I get the weirdest feeling. What he has just said doesn't really sound like a language; it's more like a kind of harsh music, or how Mum or Dad might speak if they had a mouth full of pebbles.

I ask him what it means.

"It means perhaps, '*This house was built by Eriminuha, son of Semuta, for himself and his mother.*' This wall has only been there for about one hundred years, but Eriminuha and Semuta have been dead for more than two thousand. The house they built and gave them pride vanished long ago."

"How come you can speak and read the language?"

"I am not expert. Lycian language is not well understood. But my father has interest in the history of this place and he has tried to teach me much of what he knows. Unfortunately, I am not good student. But I try."

He says that many of the smaller stones from the lost settlement that haven't been used for building have been scattered throughout the countryside. So digging can be very rewarding.

An empty garden like this is a great opportunity for him to see if he can find anything because the ground may not have been disturbed for a very long time. The fields, on the other hand, have been ploughed over so many times that there's probably no chance of finding anything worthwhile there.

With that, he starts to dig again. The ground is pale and dusty and as hard as rock. By chipping away at it with his trowel he has already dug a hole more than half a metre deep. His digging has disturbed some large red ants and he tells me to be careful because they sting.

I ask if I can help. Ali reaches into his rucksack and hands me a tool like a chisel. I kneel on the other side of the hole from him and chop at the earth with the blade of the chisel while he scoops the loosened earth out with his trowel.

As we dig, the earth changes. To begin with it looks like sand, but soon tiny orange flecks start to appear. And then, suddenly, the chisel blade hits something solid which makes a small ringing noise and jars my wrist.

My heart is racing.

Ali works his way carefully round what I've just hit, clearing away the earth and revealing a piece of pale grey stone. He slides the trowel under it and lifts it out of the hole. It's about twenty centimetres long and ten centimetres deep. As he clears the earth away from it, I can see a pattern emerging. Along the top edge there are two V-shapes and in the middle a small oval. There's no doubt about it, this is a stone that has been carved by a human at some point in the past.

I can hardly breathe.

Ali says that it's definitely Lycian. He says that it's a small piece of decoration from a building or maybe a fountain. That it's a good find.

He hands it to me and, as soon as I touch it, I can feel it all the way up my arm and through my body. It's as if it has an electrical charge. I don't really want to let go of it; it feels so good just holding it. But in the end I hand it back to Ali who dusts the remaining dirt from it.

"What will you do with it?" I ask.

"I don't know. Perhaps I will take it home to show my father."

"Is that allowed? Aren't you supposed to report it to the owner of the garden or someone?"

He looks at me and smiles. "I think this can be our secret, no?"

I smile back.

"Do you think there will be any more if we keep digging? Maybe it's part of a larger piece of stone."

"We can try."

We dig for about an hour until my arm is really aching. We find another smaller chunk of the pale grey stone but there's no carving and we find what looks like a piece of an old flower pot. Ali says that it could be part of an oil lamp but that he doesn't know enough to tell by looking at it how old it is.

"I will take it back for my father. He is student of such things. The edge is very important because is possible to learn more about how the clay was made. Sometimes it has only one colour. Sometimes it is—I think you say—speckled. Like a hen. Like a bird's egg."

He laughs.

I guess his arm must be aching as well because he stops digging at about the same time as I do. Being in the full sunshine is unbearable.

We leave the hole and move over to the trees and sit in their shade.

Ali takes a leather pouch with a silver neck and stopper out of his rucksack. He undoes the stopper, holds the bottle above his head and squeezes it. A thin jet of water squirts out and into his mouth. He drinks for a while and then hands the bottle to me. I hold it up. I squeeze it and a jet of water hits me on the nose. Ali laughs and laughs. I try again. The water is cold, even though his rucksack has been in the sun.

We lie back and look at the sky. Three hawks are quartering the garden at the speed of light. They are very thin and their wings are swept so far back that they remind me of the group of stars I can see from my bedroom window. Even when they fly directly over us, we can't hear them. Flying doesn't seem to require much effort. No flapping, just the occasional flick of their wings when they need to change direction.

Suddenly, Ali sits up: "Would you like to see other things I have found?"

He pulls a wooden box—about the size of a shoebox—from his rucksack and opens the lid. He takes out twenty or so little tiles, about a centimetre square—red, white and black. He says that they must have come from a mosaic floor. There are also a number of fragments of pottery, a bit like the one we found this morning.

And there are two small silver coins. One of them is rubbed smooth on one side but on the other it's just possible to make out the image of a man riding a winged horse.

Ali says the rider is Bellerophon and the winged horse is Pegasus. He tells me that Bellerophon killed the Chimera—a fire-breathing monster with a lion's head, a goat's body and a serpent's tail. He killed her either by firing arrows at her from Pegasus's back or by choking her to death with molten lead on the end of his spear. Ali says it depends on which version you believe.

Both versions make me feel almost sorry for the poor old Chimera. I want to say that it is just a story and that one version of a story is as good as another and that belief has nothing to do with it. But Ali talks though as though these stories are real.

The other coin is less eroded and I can quite clearly see a man's head with some sort of skin round it. Ali says that the figure is Herakles wearing a lion headdress. He says that the seated figure on the other side holding an eagle and some kind of wand is Zeus, chief of the gods. The coin was made in the time of Alexander the Great. Ali says that some people think the face of Herakles is Alexander's own. I can just make out Alexander's name running round the edge of the coin.

Αλέξανδρος

Both coins are objects of terrific power. As I hold them, my fingers tremble uncontrollably, my mind spins. And even when I hand them back to Ali, I can still feel their weight. Their solidity.

Ali and I talk for a while but then I say I'm going to have to get back to the villa for lunch.

We make our way to the broken gate together. Ali asks me to go first and check that there's no one around. But the road is empty. He says that he will be back here tomorrow and I say that I would like to help. He says that he is going to meet his father in the village. Just before we separate—me uphill, him downhill—he hands me the first piece of stone that we found and says, "This is for you."

I try to protest but I want it too badly to risk him changing his mind, so my protests aren't very effective. It is beautiful and wonderful and magical.

When I get back to the villa, Mum and Dad are preparing lunch. I don't tell them about Ali or the digging or the piece of rock, because I have a feeling that they would not approve and that they might try to get me to give it back. And there's no way I want to do that. So, I don't say anything and put it on the shelf in the dining area near the window along with a couple of other ornaments and a similar piece of stone which Mr Basak must have put there. That way no one is likely to start asking me any awkward questions.

Happiness

In fact, I didn't go back to the garden today to meet Ali because Dad suddenly decided that an outing was called for.

At breakfast he said that he felt that unlikely and badly-kept inter-generational Australian family secrets were as much of a threat to his masculinity as granny's gin and orange. That the prospect of spending another morning by the pool in the company of ancient Aunt Elspeth and young Louisa (who is no better than she should be) filled him with despair.

You certainly couldn't accuse Dad of understating or making light of things.

Mum said that she had shot, stabbed and beaten up so many people yesterday that she had needed an extra shower last night. She had even used an axe on someone and had blood on her hands and could identify strongly with Lady Macbeth.

Dad said better Lady Macbeth than Lady Macbeth's dippy old maiden aunt with all those incriminating letters that she really should have burnt still hidden in her bureau.

At this point, I stopped listening.

Mum said, "I don't suppose you fancy a rerun of the Stratonikeia trip?"

Dad said that he would rather stick pins in his eyes and that maybe we could have a day without culture.

"Where's the nearest decent beach, which is to say, unlike

the beach we went to the other day?"

They checked the map in the guidebook, which gave Dad the chance to go on about how useless it was and wonder how people were expected to get around this place.

Mum said that she'd been reading the visitors' book and that there was a beach about an hour away that was supposed to be lovely. Eventually, they found it on the useless map—it was right at the end of a thin finger of land sticking out into the sea, just where the fingernail would be.

Even Dad had to admit that the drive there was beautiful, although the going was slow because the road was so bad— nothing more really than a long series of sharp bends that hugged the side of the mountains above the flashing sea.

The people who'd written in the visitors' book said that there were lots of perfect little coves along the way. But if there were, we didn't have any luck finding them. We stopped a couple of times at likely places but couldn't find a path down to the sea; the ground was too steep and too brambly.

As we slowly wound round one corner after another, we passed through a couple of tiny villages with maybe eight or ten houses and neat orchards of oranges and olives. One village had a tiny shop with a sign which said 'Confused Grocer'.

Dad said that would be good place for him because he always felt like a confused customer.

The journey seemed to have been going on for a long time. Dad started wondering if the place even existed or whether it was a trick played on tourists. We passed through another village and past a shipbuilding yard with the skeletons of several large ships.

The road climbed steeply and when it finally leveled out we could see in front of us a huge bay that must be six or seven kilometres from one side to the other. No sooner had Mum shouted hooray, than the road turned sharply inland and uphill again and the bay vanished. Dad groaned. Ten minutes later the road turned seawards and downhill and the bay came into view again, only much closer this time.

Eventually we came to a booth in the middle of the road with a barrier across one side, but there was no one in it so we drove in on the other side.

Between us and the sea was a long row of trees with their trunks painted white. Underneath a few of them, hugging the shade, were Turkish families having barbecues. The smoke from the barbies drifted up through the branches of the trees.

On the land side—towards the mountains we'd just driven over—was a collection of huts and houses all of which looked like they'd been built by someone who knew almost nothing about building houses but had once skim read a book about how to build a shed. They were put together out of bits and pieces—planks of wood, sheets of hardboard, breeze blocks, roofing felt, plastic sheeting, oil drums. They were painted all kinds of wild colours—orange, yellow, pink, pale blue, purple. Many of the houses had verandas with old, battered armchairs and sofas. All of them had metal chimneys sticking up through the roof. The gardens were stuffed with flowers and shrubs. Most of them had flagpoles on which the Turkish flag hung limply. There were loads of butterflies and dragonflies in them but no people.

And there was hardly anyone on the beach either. Just a couple, fully clothed, watching the sea.

Dad parked the car on the sand and as we climbed out we met an old man and a little girl stepping ashore from a small fishing boat. She was carrying some small fish hung on a loop of string. He smiled at us. She smiled and held the fish up for us to admire (the fish were not smiling). They (the people not the fish) walked off the way we had just come.

Mum and Dad started talking about what a brilliant place this was. Dad said it was worth the journey, that the view was spectacular, that there were no other tourists here, that it looked like some sort of hippy commune, that it was 'louche' and 'raffish' and 'tumbledown' and 'about a million times more interesting than that beach with the waterfall and fully-clothed swimmers'. Mum agreed with everything he said.

There was absolutely nothing happening on this beach. It was just there. And yet they loved it.

Mum said, "Well if we're planning to stay here, we'll need something to eat and drink."

We wandered up the beach and found a rickety café that was even less well made than the houses. It looked seriously fragile. Like it had been built by a child. A child with very poor spatial awareness. A child without many tools and zero experience of building anything.

A wooden veranda ran across the front and there was a vine growing through the roof trellis. The light was dim inside. Mum called hello and eventually a man appeared behind the counter.

He was middle-aged and had long grey hair tied up in a scarf, a huge black moustache and gold hoops in both ears. All he needed was an eye patch. I couldn't help wondering if all the men around here feel the need to dress up as pirates.

Surprisingly, Dad said to Mum, "I'll do the ordering. You're not the only one who can speak Turkish, you know."

He turned to the guy behind the bar and proudly said, "*Iki birra lutfen.*"

The bloke behind the bar said, "So, you're from England. I used to work in a Turkish restaurant in Woking. Do you know it? Very nice place. Lovely people. My wife's from that part of the world."

Dad looked a bit miffed, after all he had just used his best Turkish on someone who spoke perfect English. But his expression changed again when a large beer was plonked down in front of him. I asked for lemonade.

The pirate said that business was very quiet because the season hadn't started properly yet.

"There's not much on the menu, I'm afraid. But I could rustle up some kind of a salad and I could cook you *pide*, which is like a Turkish pizza. Very authentic. I've got some sunbeds, which we can set up outside and I'll bring your food out to you."

The sunbeds and cushions were kept in a shed next to the café. The beds were a bit rickety (although not as rickety as the café) and the cushions smelt of mould and were covered in suspicious stains. But, as Mum and Dad agreed, the place was beautiful and none of this mattered, although in some circumstances it would.

"Besides," said Dad, "no Turkish disco."

The pirate put the beds under a parasol made of woven reeds. This was coming to bits and let the sun through in places. But even this didn't seem to phase them. Mum said that it let through 'a lovely dappled light'.

So we stayed there all afternoon and nothing really happened, although the couple who had been watching the sea so carefully, finally got changed into their swimming things and lay on sunbeds nearby. For a while they played music on one of their phones—Turkish disco naturally. But they played it so quietly that we could only just hear it. And even this didn't spoil the afternoon and they didn't play it for very long.

The only other thing to say was that there was a brilliant sunset. A huge cloud the shape of a blacksmith's anvil spread across the sky as the sun disappeared into the water in a blaze of red and gold and purple. The first few stars were hanging over the sea by the time we got back to the car.

Oh, and it's probably also worth saying that for the whole of the afternoon, the three of us were perfectly happy.

Maintaining the organism

While we were at the beach today, we watched a tiny, skinny, black and white cat picking her way—at least, I think it was a her—daintily along the sand, searching among the stones. Every so often she stopped and sniffed at a dead crab or starfish or something equally unspeakable. Having finally found a crab that wasn't too putrid, she sat down and ate it. She didn't have the appearance of enjoying it. How could she? But she obviously needed to eat and this crab, however horrible, was a source of protein.

You'd have to be pretty hungry to do that.

She was so tiny—just a scrap—that she was hardly there at all. She looked no more than a few months old. And yet her determination to survive was obviously fierce. She was just doing what her instincts tell her but, even so, I was full of admiration for her. I don't think my instinct to survive is anything like so strong. I'm not sure that it ever was.

It's the same with the cat back at the villa. Despite Steve's objections, I did buy some cat biscuits. I'm hiding them from Elif in case she reports back to Kemal who is bound to try to chase the cat away or worse.

When I gave it the biscuits for the first time, it looked suspiciously at them for a full minute before gulping them down without crunching them, swallowed them whole.

As soon as it finished eating, it looked at me as if it didn't have a care in the world. It might have been starving five minutes before, but now its belly was full.

It ambled over to where Steve was lying by the pool. It tried to climb onto his sunbed but he shouted at it and it withdrew to a safe distance, looking at him with pity and contempt.

When I lay down it looked into my eyes in its unnerving way—I never knew cats did that. Thought it was just dogs. And in its eyes was the knowledge that I wouldn't chase it away. It spoke to me and what it said was 'please'. It climbed onto my lounger, rubbed itself against my legs for a moment, curled up with its back against me and seemed to fall asleep on the instant

Given the state of its fur, I wanted to brush it away, but something stopped me.

Steve said, "Get rid of the horrible thing."

But I didn't want to disturb it. Part of me was touched to be needed by it even though I know that it is indifferent to me other than as a source of food and protection. And after a bit, I got used to it being there. I could feel it twitching in its sleep. Its warmth and softness worked a kind of magic on me and I dozed off even though I can never sleep in the afternoon.

I woke with a start and looked down. The cat had gone. Slipped away like a ghost.

Rock tomb

Because I hadn't turned up yesterday I wondered if Ali might not be there today. But I could hear him digging before I climbed through the broken door into the garden.

He was working in a patch of ground near the trees like fountains. He had cleared the plants away and had dug a larger hole than before—about a metre square and almost a metre deep. His hair was stuck to his forehead with the effort. I could see that there were more of those orange flecks and fragments in the dirt.

He showed me the morning's findings—three chunks of terracotta that, he said, could have come from anything from an oil lamp to a large jar for storing wine or olive oil. He told me to look closely at one of the pieces and I could just make out two letters which had been scratched onto it. They looked like a capital 'H' and a capital 'Z'. Ali said that he thought that they were the Greek letters eta and zeta.

I asked if he thought it was someone's name.

"Is possible, but is possible also that it is code. I have found such things before. The letter eta can mean something that is shown. Zeta reminds of a strike of lightning. So it could perhaps happen that those two letters mean what is revealed by the god of lightning—Zeus. Is possible this was an offering for a shrine.

But, of course, there may have been other letters which would give different meaning. I do not know."

As he was speaking, I looked at Ali's face and there was a very faraway look in his eyes. It was as though his attention was turned inwards, that he was seeing not a ruined garden but a busy city in which people made offerings at shrines and wrote secret messages on them to please the gods and to make their prayers extra persuasive. Maybe he was feeling some of the same things that I was feeling the other day when I held that piece of grey stone with the pattern on it. That sense of time collapsing in on itself. Like a piece of paper being folded again and again, first one way, then another.

Of course, I wasn't sure how much of what he said I should believe. It sounded like it should be true but he is very young to have studied these things. Maybe he's just repeating things he's heard his father say. Maybe he's got them wrong.

I realized that both times I'd met Ali I'd had this feeling about him: that although he is clever and precise about the objects he digs up, there is something vague and hard to define about him. That he exists as much in a world that has been dead for thousands of years as he does today. That he is not properly connected to the here and now. As though he has come loose in time and is just drifting about. I know that doesn't make a lot of sense and it's probably just that he's shy and speaking in a foreign language but it is a bit weird.

I noticed that when we talk, he looks in my direction rather than at me. Apart from that first minute when we met, we'd never made proper eye contact. It's as though he's focused on something just over my shoulder or just above my head.

Anyway, the digging was really fun. We worked on it for a couple of hours—stopping occasionally for a squirt of water. But we didn't find much; only some black splinters that might have been burnt timbers.

Eventually, we gave it up for the day and lay in the shade of the trees with our hands behind our heads, staring at the unbelievably blue sky. To our right, one of the huge white birds was climbing its spiral staircase of air until it was so high that we could hardly see it. Then it turned and drifted inland, travelling incredibly fast, carried by the winds up there.

Ali handed me the fragment of pottery with the two letters scratched on it. For all I know it might not be an offering to the gods. It could be something as ordinary as a piece of a flowerpot or a vase that some ancient Lycian lent to one of his neighbours to grow herbs in, having first scratched his name on it to make sure he got it back when they'd finished with it. But, even if that's the case, it's so old that it doesn't really matter.

"It is for you."

"It's very kind of you but I can't accept this. You gave me the carved stone you found the other day."

"It is custom to give gifts. I wish you to have it."

Just as before, I discovered that I desperately wanted it, so I graciously accepted and put it in my pocket. I wanted to go on saying no but somehow I couldn't.

Ali was wearing the same thick trousers and waistcoat as the other day. He must have been baking. I couldn't understand why he wasn't wearing shorts and a T shirt.

We talked for a while. It turned out that we are both only children. He said that he is happy to be an only child so that he

93

can be close to his father and be 'dutiful'. That seemed an odd thing to say, but I guessed I knew what he meant.

And then he said, "We are small family; just my father and myself. My mother died before I was born."

This woke me up. I thought about it for a moment and then said, "*Before* you were born?"

He laughed. "No, no. That was foolish mistake. I mean that my mother died *as* I was born. In childbirth. It has just been my father—Baba—and myself. Always. Baba says that my mother and myself passed each other going in different ways. He says it not to make joke but to make me small amount less sad when I think about her."

It suddenly seemed like a good time to change the subject. I asked him about his school in Istanbul.

Only boys go there. The masters wear long black gowns and skullcaps. And the subjects that he studies seem to focus on maths (he said 'mathematics') and literature and history.

He told me about his best friend Aleem, who he walks to school with. Sometimes Aleem's father gives them extra money and they go to a café and drink çay and watch all the glamorous people in the city's streets.

I asked him if he has a girlfriend. He looked embarrassed and his face flushed. "I do not, of course. The only ladies I speak to are my aunt—my father's sister—and our maid. And women who work in shops. To do otherwise would not be respectful."

I asked him how long he's been interested in archaeology.

"Since I was small child. My father works very hard. He is engineer. What time is left is important to him. He is scholar. I am honoured to be able to help him in small ways. It is job of son to share his father's interests."

I wasn't sure about this idea of a son's duty. Dad's interests seem to be moaning about things in general, drinking and reading novels about seven foot-tall sociopathic loners. I'm not sure how intellectually stimulating it would be for me to share them with him. Besides, I think the whole point of his interests is that he *doesn't* share them with anyone. Well, apart from the drinking bit. And not even that some of the time.

Ali tells me about their apartment in Istanbul which, he says, is dark and cool in summer and full of books. "My father likes things to be quiet so that he can study." Their cottage is very different. "It is very plain—is that how you say it?—but peaceful. There are not many other houses and we have stream that passes in front. I like very much staying here, but is not my home. Istanbul is my home. In my heart, I am a boy of the city."

The more we talked, the more unsettled and uncomfortable I became. I had this feeling that there was something that he wasn't telling me. Something he was keeping from me although I couldn't imagine why. Something really important.

And because I thought he was holding out on me I started to feel irritated with him. Almost angry. And that's not a good feeling. So, I stood up and said that I was leaving.

He looked surprisingly upset about this and stood up as well.

"Please don't leave yet. There is something that I would like to show you. Something that I have never shown anyone before. I have never told anyone about it. Not even Baba. It is my biggest secret. I would like you to know it."

"What is it?" I knew that I was behaving badly, especially given that I did really want to know. After all, the things he had shown me so far had been pretty amazing.

"I would prefer to show you. It will not take long."

"All right."

"We will have to walk to get there."

I guess it's now around five o'clock and it's still boiling. The sun is so bright that the plants in the garden look as though all the colour has been bleached out of them. Ali takes a long drink from his water bottle then hands it to me.

We follow the path back towards the villa but when we get to the cemetery in the woods we turn off down a track that I've never noticed before. Probably because it's hardly there at all. It's really nothing more than a depression in the grass, scattered with pellets of goat shit. You would never see it unless you were looking for it. We follow it through the trees. It's cooler in here and shadows dance and play on the ground.

This afternoon feels unreal. I can hardly believe that Ali and I are doing what we're doing. It's like walking in a dream. A dream in which you just accept that you might go on walking forever. That you might never arrive anywhere.

But, of course, it isn't a dream. After a bit, we pass a pine tree that is twisted and bent nearly in half and the path starts to slope steeply upwards. The undergrowth gets thicker and Ali uses a stick to clear a way through.

The further we go, the more nervous I get. It's suddenly hard to get enough air into my lungs.

As if he understands what I'm feeling, Ali turns to me and says, "We are almost there." His voice sounds very loud in the silence and stillness.

A silence that is suddenly broken by a loud, repeated

knocking noise.

I'm so nervous that it makes me jump. The noise continues. It's like pieces of wood being knocked together.

"What's that?" I ask. My throat is dry and my voice little more than a whisper.

Ali turns and smiles.

"You will see, in moment."

I'm not sure that I want to. The noise becomes louder and more insistent.

A few paces further on and Ali bends back the branch of a large bush and there on the ground are half a dozen tortoises in a circle, butting into one another.

The sense of being in a dream doesn't completely leave me but I'm so relieved that I laugh out loud. At least it's not skeletons dancing. Besides, there is something funny about tortoises. It's not so much that they move so slowly, but that they are such a ridiculous mixture of the hard and the soft.

Ali says, "The one in middle is female. Others are all male. They are trying to get under her shell. They are trying to mate with her. Is why they bump into her. Sometimes they succeed too well and turn female onto her back and she dies. She cooks in sun."

For some reason, I don't believe Ali has brought me all this way to see tortoises bonking. And I'm right. I also don't think I'd much like to be a lady tortoise.

He returns to the path and carries on up the slope, which has got even steeper. "Is not far now."

As I look at him walking ahead of me, I have this ridiculous urge to turn and run—out of the forest and back to the villa.

Huge boulders covered with cracks and seams and wrinkles have appeared on both sides of the track. The undergrowth is taller than we are and very thick.

Ali turns to me and says, "You must be careful now."

He gets down on his hands and knees and crawls into a thicket, completely disappearing from sight. I have no choice so I kneel down and follow him. The silence in here is deafening and I start to feel really claustrophobic. Fortunately, after a couple of moments we emerge onto a platform of rock, covered with scrubby grass and thistles.

It's only about three metres wide and beyond it is NOTHING.

Just space.

We're on the very top of a cliff. Below us is a steep-sided gorge at the bottom of which is a river bed full of huge boulders and a trickle of water. In the far distance is the sea. We crawl to the edge and look over. The drop is terrifying. My stomach turns over and the horizon twists and sways. Trees are growing out of the rock at crazy angles and we can see where there have been rockfalls. Between us and the sea is the main road on which tiny cars are travelling. The people in them have no idea that we are here so high above them.

This is a scary place.

And then Ali suggests that we climb down the side of the cliff.

"You have to be joking."

"No, I am serious. I will guide you. I will ensure that you are safe."

Without waiting for a reply, he moves to the side of the rock platform and starts to climb down hand over hand. I have no idea why I am following him, but it seems that I am.

In fact, once I've committed to the idea of doing something so stupid, it isn't as terrifying as I first thought, and I'm certainly hoping it isn't as dangerous as I first thought. There are some obvious handholds and places for your feet. As long as I don't look down and don't think about what I'm doing, I might even be OK.

Once we've climbed down about six or seven metres, we come to a narrow ledge, just wide enough for us to both stand on.

The rock face is partly hidden by a huge fig tree which is growing directly out of the cliff. I grab hold of it and its leathery leaves scrape my arms. Its sweet, slightly musty smell fills the air. There are thousands of tiny figs among the leaves and a scar on the trunk where one of its branches must have come off years ago.

"This is what I wanted to show you," says Ali. "This is my secret. Now is our secret."

I can't believe he has brought me all this way to see a tree. And I'm right.

I realize that there is a space behind it, a hole in the rock, just under two metres wide and the same high. It takes me a moment to notice that that is what is significant about it. It is perfectly square, which means that it has been cut out by someone, although I can't imagine who or why. This is not a cave, not a natural feature. It's man-made.

When we squeeze past the fig's trunk, I can see that whoever cut this hole also decorated it. Round its edge they've carved what looks like a door frame in the rock.

When we crawl inside it's as though we are entering someone's house through the front door.

It's baking hot in here. There's a kind of stone bench or couch carved out of the rock on one side and it even looks like whoever carved it wanted to create the impression in stone of a pillow. The floor is littered with scraps of pottery and the roof is black with soot.

My heart is just beginning to return to something like its normal rhythm when Ali says, "This is a rock tomb. A house of the dead." My heart goes back to beating at around two million beats a minute.

"Whose tomb is it?" I ask.

"I do not know. It has been here for perhaps two thousand years. I found it by luck earlier in summer. I have told no one. I ask you to keep it our secret."

I think to myself that there's no danger of me telling Mum and Dad about it. I can just imagine what they would say if they knew that I had been clambering about on a cliff without a rope. Or even *with* a rope.

Ali says that the person who was buried here must have been very important. It must have been so difficult to have got a body in here that they would only have done it for a person of great status.

"Why is the body or the remains of a body not here now?"

"I do not know. Perhaps it was eaten by animals. Perhaps turned to dust. The people who brought it here wanted the dead person to see village and fields. They made it look like house because they wanted dead person to feel at home."

"But shouldn't you tell someone about this place? Your father, maybe?"

"No. No one would come here. If they did it might be as if they were stealing something from me. Is better to keep it as secret. To keep it as special place. As *our* special place. You will promise me that?"

We sit and look out through the fig tree's branches at the world below, like we own it.

Ali seems to be thinking so hard that I can practically hear his brain clicking. He has that faraway look in his eyes again.

Thinking about Mum and Dad has made me realize that they will probably start getting worried if I don't get back soon. I say to Ali that it's time to go.

He says, "Will you promise to come back again?"

I say that I will.

We climb back up the cliff—again, I'm really careful not to think about what I'm doing or what would happen if it went wrong—and follow the path down through the woods and past the cemetery. I expect Ali to head downhill towards the village but he says that he is going back to the cottage.

It turns out that he walks all the way with me. He says that his father's cottage is further along the road that passes above our villa. I ask him if he would like to come in and meet Mum and Dad—I can hear them by the pool—but he says that he must get home.

The sun is very low in the sky and shining straight down the road. Every leaf, every pebble, every blade of grass is absolutely clear.

Ali says goodbye and hopes that we will meet again in the

garden very soon.

I start to go down the steps but then turn to watch him. I can see his back move against the fabric of his shirt, I can hear his footsteps on the track, I can see the sun on his hair, and I can see that he isn't casting a shadow.

The pickled boys

She thinks I don't know about the cat biscuits. She thinks she is being kind and I guess that if she was in England in her own house she would do exactly the same thing.

I've heard that people in England even feed foxes. It would be like us leaving food out for the wild boar or the snakes. Not that anyone would do such a thing. It would be bound to end in trouble.

Elif has reported that she has found a container near the pool that is obviously being used to feed that wretched cat. It is a beautiful animal and I feel sorry for it. But it has no future. I should have shot it last autumn when no one was around.

When they leave, there will be no food for the cat and it will either starve or come into my garden and try to kill my chickens. It may not know it but its days are numbered.

I spoke to Seyhan just before midnight. Her mother is in poor shape and, Seyhan thinks, sure to die. She will stay until this happens. I agreed that she must although who knows how long her mother will last? Here I am again, wishing ill for a woman who has never done me any harm. Whose only crime is her claim on Seyhan.

We talked, as we always do, about how things are here, how the new guests were settling in, about whether the nightingales were still singing. I told her that they were, although I fear they will not be by the time she returns. Every year their singing seems more precious and, year by year, it seems sadder when they stop.

I told her that Maggie seems to have adopted the grey, ghostly cat. But I did not mention all those ghost children who cluster around me in the house when she's not here. And, of course, I omitted to mention that my heart was breaking.

I got no sleep after our conversation and I always hate myself when this happens. A better man would get eight hours straight even if his wife had left him or he was booked for open heart surgery in the morning. I, on the other hand, sweated and tangled with the sheets and then gave up and came out here at first light. The moon was still in the sky.

Although a lot of the labour in this garden has been provided by Urfuz, the designs are mine. Seyhan likes flowers, particularly plants such as buddleias, which bring the butterflies, and lemon trees, for the scent of their blossom. But my interest has always been in succulents and cacti. They are not pretty and they don't make any concessions, but they manage to survive in the most challenging situations. They are hard and untouchable on the outside but soft and liquid on the inside. They have to flower but they do it as infrequently as is consistent with the survival of the species. But when they do it, boy do they do it. No holding back. They really go for it.

I love those scenes in the movies where a cowboy who is dying of thirst in the desert suddenly comes across a cactus. He climbs down off his horse, unfolds his knife and cuts a wedge which he then sucks to slake his thirst. Refreshed, he can continue to go after the bad guys. How many plants contributed so much to bringing justice to the Wild West?

Because Seyhan and I made this garden together, getting my hands in the earth brings me closer to her. I imagine the soil running under our garden, under the mountains, under the central plain and all the way to Ankara. If she was in the garden of her mother's nursing home and were to put her hands into the earth, it would be like we were touching one another.

We hired a small digger to excavate the hole for the pool here and found a couple of pieces of what we think are Lycian masonry. Somehow, finding them confirmed what we had felt since we first saw the site—that this was a good place to build, in spite of the difficulty of the terrain. I've put one of the pieces in *Kelebek Kirmizi* for luck and kept one in the house here. It's on the shelf next to my Agathas.

For the first few years of our marriage, Seyhan and I rented a small flat in Kinzmik which was in the process of a rapid—some might say catastrophic—transformation, from sleepy, forgotten fishing village to crowded tourist destination. The flat was pretty basic, although Seyhan always bought flowers from the market for the kitchen table.

From our tiny kitchen we had a view of the mountains behind and we could see the hang gliders hurl themselves fearlessly from the top and drift over the town to the harbour.

Sometimes there was one person on the hang glider, sometimes two. Sometimes they came so close that we could hear the wind in their sails (if that's what you call them). Sometimes it felt like they might land on the roof. Once, when a hang glider came even nearer than usual, I held a bottle of wine and a glass out of the window and asked the guy steering it if he'd like a drink. He looked at me and smiled. I would have loved it if he'd swept the glass out of my hand and touched it to his lips, before hurling it into the sea.

I used to wonder what our house would look like from the air, whether it would be possible to peek in and see us sitting at the kitchen table. Seyhan once suggested that I go to the office on the harbour and see if I could book a flight. I wouldn't have to steer it, just be strapped in. She said that she would wave to me out of the window as I flew past like Icarus. I asked her if she would hold out a glass of champagne to me as I drifted by. She said that she would be delighted. But in the end I never did it and I don't know how serious she was. After all, she knows the kind of man I am.

Because Kinzmik was expanding so rapidly, there was always legal work available, even if not much of it was very exciting. To begin with, it mainly related to planning laws. Putting up ramshackle, unlovely hotels without the necessary permissions was practically a national sport at the time. And who could blame them? The people of Kinzmik had had a pretty hard time more or less since the Romans left. But then, in the early 1980s, the road arrived and everything changed.

The municipal authorities tried to hold the line, maintain the standard of the buildings, retain a degree of authenticity, but it was always clear that they were fighting a losing battle. If people are prepared to go to prison in order to put another storey on their cheap hotel what, ultimately, can you do?

But as Kinzmik grew, other crimes started to appear: shoplifting, drunkenness, the occasional assault. For me, it was a living of sorts, even if not one I could be particularly proud of.

Although, I did once manage to help to get a closure order enforced against a multinational company that was building a hotel on a beach where turtles came to lay their eggs,

Meantime, Seyhan had a job in a rapidly growing local secondary school—a brand new building, surrounded by pines, with a view of the sea. She was happy. She believed —although I was never sure if she was right—that many of her students learned to love the classics. But I *am* sure that many of them learned to love her.

At weekends we would drive along the coast and find little bays to swim in, although that was getting increasingly difficult to do and sometimes our peace would be shattered by the arrival of a tourist boat playing rock music at ear-bursting volume. On occasions, the people on the boats showed us their bums.

Sometimes we would drive over the mountains to visit the site of Ancient Myra, where they were excavating the high rise, honeycomb of rock tombs and the Roman theatre. Someone—I can't remember who, although Seyhan would know—said that the rock tombs reminded them of the mullioned widows of an Elizabethan manor house in England.

Seyhan said that this place was home to many stories.

Stories, for example, about Myrrha, the mother of Adonis, whose own mother used to compare her beauty with that of Aphrodite. Miffed, Aphrodite caused Myrrha to fall in love and commit incest with her father, the king of Cyprus. When he discovered this, he pursued her with an axe. Aphrodite intervened and turned her into a tree. Adonis was born from its trunk and his mother's tears fell as droplets of aromatic resin.

She said that the forested slopes nearby were equally full of myths and memories: of the Chimera whose flame, some say, can still be seen on still nights; of Antony giving a love gift of timber from the forests of Oenium to Cleopatra for her navy; of Alexander's soldiers seeking a way north to Xanthus.

And she told me that, according to Homer, it was from the Solymi mountains just south of Myra that Poseidon spotted Odysseus when he left Calypso's island and his dream of endless, consequence-free sex. (She advised me not to get any ideas.) Poseidon, just back from a trip to Ethiopia, was furious and sent a terrible storm to wreck Odysseus.

Or we'd go to Demre where they had recently dug the underground church of Saint Nicholas with its beautiful frescoes of the life of the saint out of hundreds of years' worth of alluvial silt. This was before the Russians came.

In my favourite fresco Saint Nicholas—looking remarkably serene—is being rowed through a storm in an open boat. Two of the oarsmen look as though they anticipate disaster. What the third was thinking is impossible to say since his head is missing.

Seyhan said that what she liked about Saint Nicholas was that he wasn't a snob. In fact, he was positively promiscuous in his choice of causes. After all, he was the patron saint of children, virgins, merchants, pawnbrokers, sailors, scholars, thieves and those unjustly imprisoned. Among the cast iron, definitely-did-happen, no-doubt-about-it miracles attributed to him were raising the dead, preventing shipwrecks, recovering lost property, parting a swollen river and escaping unscathed from a collapsing church.

She told me a story about the saint and some pickled boys. She said that he once stopped at an inn where other travelers were having supper. They invited him to join them but he stopped them from eating because he recognized that what was being served was the flesh of three boys who had been murdered in their sleep, cut up and pickled by the local butcher. Saint Nicholas told the boys to put on their flesh once again and in that instant they were resurrected and assumed their bodily form. She said that the story went that they came back to life singing 'Alleluiah', but she rather doubted this. She said that, given her knowledge of boys gained from her years of teaching, they would have been more likely to say something like, "Never mind 'Alleluiah', we're going to cut that fucking butcher's fucking balls off with one of his own fucking knives." She said that seeing the boys emerging out of the stew must have been like seeing three strippers bursting out of a cake.

Sometimes she would take a dish from the oven and put it on the table saying, "Pickled boys, with the compliments of St Nick."

Testudinidae

It is not easy for me to ask my children for help. It always feels like a failure. Like a reversal of the correct order of things. I am their father. It is for me to protect and guide *them*. To show wisdom. But they are cleverer than me—they have their mother's brains (not that I would ever admit it to her; a man must fake superiority in his marriage even when he does not truly feel it). And, of course, they are comfortable with technology in a way that I can never be. The truth is that I am afraid of computers. Afraid of the internet.

But asking for help from Selim was the lesser of two evils.

I have been unable to get the tortoise that shits by the pool out of my head. It is as if it has built a nest in my brain. When I close my eyes to sleep, it lumbers insolently across my inner eye. It's there as well in my dreams, grown huge. And when it reappeared after all those weeks, having travelled several kilometres and climbed more than three hundred metres, I was a little bit afraid. I felt helpless. I want it gone but it seems determined to stay.

They say that one should know one's enemy, so I decided to find out as much about it as I could.

Naturally, Selim's first question was why I should want to use his laptop. "You know you don't like it, Dad. Do you even know how to use it? What do you want to look up? Let me do it for you."

For some reason, I was reluctant to mention the tortoise to him, so I said that I thought it was about time I joined what I have heard described on TV as 'the cyber generation' (he laughed) and found out more about how these things work. That I wasn't yet ready to become some kind of relic left behind by the future. I could tell that he didn't believe me and I saw Elif rolling her eyes at him. It occurred to me afterwards that she may have thought that I wanted to watch pornography.

Anyway, Selim logged me in and left me to it. He said to key in what I wanted to know about and follow the links. This proved less difficult than I feared, even though I can type only with one finger.

The first thing I discovered was that the brain of the tortoise is extremely small. This was not a great surprise, although, to be fair, its direction finding abilities must be considerable. And small though it is, it seems that the tortoise does not use much of it. I read about a man called Francesco Redi, who conducted experiments in the seventeenth century. To begin with, he removed the brain of a land tortoise that then lived for a further six months. Next he decapitated a tortoise (I was unable to find out whether it was the same one or another) which lived comfortably enough for twenty three days without a head. I assume it died of starvation. When he did the same with fresh-water tortoises the results were similar, although they did not live as long.

This all seemed very unlikely to me. How could anything live without a head?

I was distracted enough to spend a few moments discovering

more about this Redi person. Turns out he was a physician, naturalist, biologist and *poet,* who wrote a very long poem in praise of Tuscan wines. Which may explain a lot about his crazy experiments.

The next thing I found was a video of a Japanese man walking a huge tortoise through the streets of Tokyo as if it were a dog. Oddly enough, the man himself looks quite a lot like a tortoise. Its name is Bon-chan and it weighs seventy kilos. I am very glad there are no tortoises such as this in Turkey.

I also learned that the tortoise is a symbol of the Greek god Hermes. This is very hard to understand. I remember when I was at school Mrs Basak taught us about Hermes. She said that he had winged sandals and was the messenger of the gods. So, what could he possibly have to do with a clumsy, useless animal such as a tortoise?

But then, it seems, that many things about the tortoise are contradictory. For the ancient Greeks and Romans, it was a symbol of fertility. It is beyond me to see a tortoise as a sex symbol. They are slow creatures, unsatisfactory, unlovely. I have more sympathy with the Chinese who apparently describe a man whose wife sleeps with another as 'wearing a green hat', which means that he is like a tortoise. The tortoise is like a man who is not a man.

I also found a story about a tortoise and a scorpion. For some reason they were both standing on the banks of a river which they needed to cross. The scorpion couldn't swim and asked the tortoise if he could ride on its back. The tortoise was reluctant because he feared that the scorpion would sting him, but the scorpion promised that he wouldn't. "What would be the point?

We would both die." So in the end, the tortoise agreed. The scorpion climbed on his back and they set off. But when they got to the middle of the river, the scorpion lashed its sting and pierced the tortoise's neck. "Why did you do that?" asked the tortoise as his legs weakened and his eyesight started to fade, "now we are both going to die." "I know," said the scorpion, "I just couldn't help myself. It's in my nature to sting. That's what I do." As the tortoise died he sank, taking the scorpion with him. Their bodies were washed all the way to the sea.

This story confused me. I didn't know what to feel about it. What did it mean? I couldn't see the point of it. Was it trying to tell me something? But I can't help wondering if a scorpion could really kill a tortoise...

While I had been on Selim's computer, I had not noticed the time passing. Eventually, he asked if he could have it back because he had homework still to do, although I am certain he was using it to watch football. I could hear the cheering through his bedroom door.

My head was spinning. It was full of useless information about tortoises. The evening had been a failure. I had learned nothing that enabled me to sort out my feelings about this creature. Nothing that would help me deal with it.

And, of course, when I fell asleep at last, I dreamed of a huge, decapitated tortoise clanking to the poolside and shitting enormously by the pool. I shouted at it to stop and tried to chase it away. It took no notice. I thought of picking it up and hurling it down the hillside but realized that it was too heavy for me to lift. And even though it didn't have a head, I knew that there was a smirk of satisfaction on its face.

John Melmoth

The language of the stars

I need to think about what I saw—or, I suppose, what I *didn't* see—yesterday. The fact—if it is a fact—that Ali doesn't have a shadow. He seems to be as solid as I am and yet apparently there was nothing to stop the sun passing straight through him.

Can it mean that he isn't really there? That I'm imagining him? But that's obviously ridiculous. And besides, if I was imagining him I would easily be able to imagine a shadow for him. Just to keep my imaginings nice and consistent and tidy.

The obvious explanation is that he *does* have a shadow—just like everyone else. I couldn't see it yesterday because of a trick of the light (the sun was dazzling). Or maybe I'd had too much sun. I guess that has to be it. At least, I almost guess that has to be it.

But, either way, I don't feel ready to meet him again just yet. So I won't be going back to the garden today.

Instead, something is telling me to go back to the tomb on the cliff face. I'm not sure what that something is but I seem to be following orders.

The trouble is that when I get back to the cemetery I can't find the path that we took yesterday. I'm pretty sure that I know roughly where it was but without Ali to point it out I can't locate it. So, I step into the trees and immediately lose any sense

114

of direction. At once, I'm close to panic. I crash around for a couple of moments but then I see the doubled-over pine tree.

I still can't find any path but I know that I have to head upwards through the shrubs, which seem to have grown back since Ali and I crawled through them. And then, quite suddenly, here I am at the top of the world. I look down and wish I hadn't. The enormous space in front of me seems to be calling and I have to use all my willpower not to jump.

I stand here with my eyes closed, breathing hard. But then I climb down to the fig tree (still taking care not to give a moment's thought to what's going on) and pull myself into the hole. I sit on the floor with my eyes closed.

A rustling noise makes me open them again and there against the wall in the corner is a large snake with a zigzag pattern down the length of its body. The problem is that I'm between it and the mouth of the tomb.

Without thinking, I jump backwards towards the entrance and almost fall. I just manage to grab one of the fig tree's branches at the very last moment.

My sudden movement panics the snake which tries to escape through the back of the hole and then turns and comes straight for me, hissing angrily. I lift my right foot and it slithers past me and down into a crack in the rock. It's gone.

I climb back into the tomb and sit on the stone couch among all those bits of broken pottery. I think I nearly died. Possibly twice. I feel like crying. The sweat is running off me. My heart is beating at a rate I didn't know it was capable of.

I still have no idea why I've come here but, in spite of everything, I start to relax. I sit with my knees under my chin and look through the fig tree's branches at the world beyond. For such a dangerous place, it feels oddly safe, as long as there aren't any snakes in it.

And that's when the visions or hallucinations or whatever they are begin. The entrance to the tomb is suddenly like a cinema screen with images rushing past, although I guess those images could just as easily be in my head.

In fact, I hear something before I see anything: a scrabbling noise above and the murmur of voices. I just have time to notice that the branches of the fig tree have disappeared before two lengths of crudely-made rope appear in front of me, dangling in space.

A moment later a pair of brown legs comes into sight, swiftly followed by the rest of a young guy—not much older than me—in a white tunic and no shoes. He swings into the hole. I crouch as far back as I can in the corner. I don't really have time to think how embarrassing this is going to be and how I'm going to explain why I'm here, when it becomes clear that he can't see me. And either he doesn't take up any room or I don't because he's able to move around in this small space without ever coming into contact with me.

He hangs onto the rope and leans back over the drop and calls up, presumably to people above. A couple of minutes later, the second rope starts to move and another guy in the same kind of tunic comes into sight. Both then lean back out of the tomb and call up. Their words are really harsh. It sounds like they're made entirely of consonants. Like they're speaking barbed wire.

I can hear small stones sliding down the rock face. Two more ropes appear and tied to them is a bundle, the size of a man, wrapped in thick cloth. A voice from above calls down. They each grab a rope with one hand, lean back over the drop as though they have no fear of heights, and with the other hand grasp the bundle, which they swing into the tomb.

I can hear women crying. The bundle takes up a lot of the space in here, so the two guys have to kneel on the ledge outside and reach in. They untie the ropes from the bundle and the ropes are pulled up.

They shift the bundle onto the stone couch. I notice that there are no broken pieces of crockery on the floor any more. There are paintings of wildflowers on the walls, paintings that weren't here a moment ago.

Another much smaller bundle comes down on a fifth rope. They open it and pull out armfuls of olive branches and wildflowers and herbs which they scatter round the inside of the tomb. And, finally, they arrange three clay pots, decorated with crude paintings of octopus and starfish, around the bundle. They are open at the top and have something in them which smells very strong and sweet. Like pine trees.

When everything has been arranged as they want it, they again grab the ropes and face outwards. With their free hands they touch their foreheads and their chests where their hearts are. They then say some bizarre words very clearly and slowly. Like they are casting a spell but I guess it's a prayer of some sort. The crying and wailing from above get louder.

Finally, they hang onto their ropes with both hands, call up to the people at the top and climb or are pulled out of sight.

I'm left alone with the bundle. The smell of whatever's in the pots is so powerful it's making me dizzy.

Then things accelerate. Night follows day follows night follows day follows night, until they are a blur. Light and dark, dark and light, light and dark, faster and faster. Days, weeks, years, centuries strobe by in a flash.

The entrance to the tomb is a window on the sky. By day, clouds—sometimes white, sometimes purple—grow huge, collapse and disappear. Wind howls, rain streams down, lightning crackles, the sun burns and occasionally a blizzard blows up. All in the blink of an eye. Eclipses momentarily darken the world. The sun ripens hundreds of years' of crops in the time it takes to think it.

By night the stars burn and change their positions in the sky with the speed of a stop-motion film. And I have learned to read the language of the stars.

All year round, Cassiopeia, in love with her own beauty, and Draco, the dragon, and Ursa, the great bear, rule the skies. In spring there is Hydra the serpent, and Bootes, the herdsman. In summer Cygnus the swan drifts southwards, Saggitarius, the centaur, points his great bow, Lyra plucks her lyre and sings. In the autumn Andromeda—who triggered the wrath of the monstrous Cetus—rises, Aquarius the water carrier travels the horizon. In winter, Orion hunts on the banks of Eriadnus, the heavenly river.

Stories as old as time are told in the sky.

The story of how Apollo sent a crow to fetch water from a local spring so that he could make a sacrifice to Zeus. When the crow lied Apollo exiled him to the night skies along with Crater—the cup from which the gods drink—and Hydra. Hydra had instructions always to stay between the bird and the cup so that Corvus must remain eternally thirsty.

The story of Pegasus the winged horse, foaled from the blood of Medusa, who took on the colour of the sea's foam and who was installed by Zeus among the stars.

Or the story of Herakles who strangled two snakes while still in his crib and now patrols the sky accompanied by Cerebus his three-headed dog.

There are meteor showers and falling stars, comets that hang in the sky for months on end, and unimaginable explosions in deepest space which light up a corner of the heavens before dwindling to nothing.

A wash of pale moonlight flickers constantly across the tomb's floor.

And while this happening, the bundle shrinks and changes, collapses in on itself. The cloth pales in the sun and is stripped off by the wind, leaving a skull and a pile of bleached bones. Then the bones turn to dust, which is carried away into the sky.

The wall paintings start to fade like real wildflowers. Soon they are nothing more than a ghostly image—a memory—and then they are gone.

And all this time, no one comes, although animals do. Snakes and lizards and scorpions live out their lives here. Spiders spin their webs across the mouth of the tomb and the silk of their webs catches the setting sun. Goats scramble past and occasionally poke their heads in. Rats and foxes explore the space and find it not to their liking. Generations of bats roost on the roof and then, inexplicably, are gone. The shit with which they have coated the floor turns to dust and disappears on the wind.

Across the generations, kestrels and peregrines make their homes here. And once, a pair of eagles raises chicks in a terrible nest—scarcely more that a bundle of sticks—on the tomb's floor. The adult birds bring back a hare, a baby goat, pigeons, a huge fish. The three ugly chicks pounce on their parents' prey, tearing it to pieces. While they are in occupation, the tomb is filthy and stinks, crawls with mites and fleas. But no sooner have the chicks fledged than the ravens come and strip things clean, carrying off the sticks for their own nests, croaking in triumph and spite. The parent birds do not have the energy to fight for continued possession and never come again.

The spiders resume their endless work of spinning in the tomb's mouth. Trees come and go. They reach for the sky for an instant and then fall. The grass and the weeds grow and ripen and die.

And then, at last, someone comes.

A mad face appears at the opening and I can't help but flinch. It is the face of a fierce, insane hermit, filthy and bedraggled, hair and beard down to his waist, a skeleton in a thin envelope of skin. Another bag of bones.

He sweeps the floor with brushwood and keeps dead insects in the pots. He lives on wild fruits, wild honey and locusts, which he eats raw. Lizards when he can catch them. Just enough to keep his body alive. He drinks rainwater. He spends his days lashing himself with branches and praying to whoever his god is. At night, he lies on the hard floor muttering incessantly in his sleep. And then, as suddenly as he arrived he is gone. Maybe dead, maybe gone on some crazy pilgrimage somewhere.

The seasons follow one another. Spring, summer, autumn,

winter and then again and again and again. The stars wheel past. A single glorious butterfly lands just inside the hole, its wings fold in and out.

And then—maybe it's a day, maybe it's a thousand years later—a soldier arrives, fleeing from some war or other. His uniform is in rags and his hair is tangled. There is blood on his cheek. I can feel his fear, his sense of helplessness. He smashes the pots to make a hearth on which he cooks a rabbit he has snared. As he eats, he thinks of home and the tears run down his filthy cheeks. He stays a week or two, or maybe it's just a millionth of a second. He leaves. Who knows what happened to him? Whether or not he ever got home, whether he was caught and punished as a deserter.

And then, finally, a boy who looks a lot like Ali comes. He is wearing thick black trousers and a black waistcoat. He comes often, spending whole days at a time sitting on the ledge, his legs dangling in space, perhaps thinking about the mother he never knew, perhaps thinking about his father, perhaps thinking about his friend Aleem, perhaps thinking about his future.

The fig tree is back again, shading the hole, but it is not much more than a sapling.

It is getting dark, the boy who looks a lot like Ali is preparing to leave, but he has become careless and trips. He saves himself by gripping the fig tree, just as I did. For a moment his heart settles, but then the branch snaps and he starts to fall. I leap to the front of the tomb and try to catch him. I stretch out my arm and touch the tips of his fingers. Our eyes lock as he falls further and further, back into the world, back out of the world.

There is fear in his eyes but also acceptance. He falls as far and as fast as a star. I can do nothing to stop it. And I know that however many times I come here in the future, I will never be able to do anything to stop it.

That I will always fail to catch him; that he will always fall.

That he can never be saved...

I must have slept. I'm stiff and cold. The night is black but the stars are blazing. Not just silver but red and green and gold, and colours that I have never seen before—the colours that are created where orange meets purple, where blue collides with silver. I can see the lights of the village and the lights of the cars on the road. I know that I have to go back to the villa and that means that I have to make the climb in the dark.

But before I go, there is one thing I have to do: I pick up a broken piece of pottery and use it to scratch my name on the wall.

Matt

It's so dark in here that I can't see it, but I know it's there.

And that makes me feel better.

Makes me feel real and solid after that terrifying blur of time and change.

A fine bromance

For a change, I was up before Maggie this morning. I left her sleeping and had a wander round the garden. Urfuz had just finished the pool and we smiled before he scuttled off to wherever he scuttles off to. To do whatever it is he does—cook crystal meth, wax his moustache, give his missus a good seeing to. Who knows?

Anyway, I was sitting at the dining table when who should wander past but Kemal? He was obviously surprised to see me so early. We both smiled a little awkwardly but, unlike his employee, he didn't scuttle off.

He was obviously keen to talk so we chatted about this and that. I'm not taken in by that schtick of his about how much he misses his wife. He obviously doesn't want anyone to believe it, but my guess is he's as pussy-whipped as the next man.

Anyway, the upshot of our little talk was that he invited me over for a drink this evening. I said that I would only come if he promised not to offer me raki, and he said that shouldn't be too much of a problem. I then said that I would only come if he had some proper tonic water. He said that shouldn't be too much of a problem either.

What *was* more of a problem was that the invitation was obviously for me alone. That what he was hoping for was a manly *tête-à-tête*. Personally, I can't think of anything worse,

123

but, given that he'd promised tonic, I felt I had to say yes.

I thought Maggie would go ballistic when I told her that I didn't think she'd been invited. But, instead, she thought it was funny.

"No," she said, "it's quite all right. I'd only be in the way." And she seemed to think that was pretty funny too. Naturally, I gave her the stern face treatment.

So, anyway, this evening, I went. You get to Kemal's garden through an old fashioned wooden door in the wall just beyond the pool. There was no bell or knocker so I pulled it open. He's got a lovely courtyard garden and loads of chickens looking kind of decorative.

Kemal was sitting at a little table smoking an enormous cigar and he greeted me like a long-lost relative, telling me how delighted he was to welcome me to his house.

I said something memorable like, "That's very kind of you."

He asked me if I'd like a cigar and looked so disappointed when I said that I didn't smoke that I almost wished I did. He thought this over for a moment and then asked me if I would like to try a local drink. He didn't think there was an English equivalent for its name. The best he could come up with was 'gin and tonic'.

I said that I was willing give it a try. "I am on holiday, after all, and open to new experiences. 'Gin and tonic', is that the correct pronunciation?"

He said that it was then disappeared inside the house and came back a few moments later with a tray on which there was a bottle of Plymouth gin (how brilliant is that?), two bottles of tonic, two glasses, a jar of sliced lemons and a bowl of nibbles that looked like seeds in sawdust.

He poured the gin and then extracted two slices of lemon from the jar. I could see from the label that it was shop bought. Only a man with several lemon trees in his garden would ever think about buying such a thing. If I ruled the world, I'd make it a crime not to use a lemon you'd just picked from the tree you were sitting under.

It reminded me of my uncle Charles, a very good chum of Dorothy. After a spectacularly unsuccessful career as a merchant banker he decided to retire, aged fifty, to the Amalfi Coast, where he had always dreamed of building his own villa. I think his bosses would have been happy to give him twice the money to go away. Their only concern would have been whether or not the Amalfi Coast was far enough to prevent him doing any further harm. Anyway, he gave his architect pretty free rein; the only thing he really insisted on was that the floors were to be of marble. He said that ever since he'd been a schoolboy—even then he was a fan of light opera—he had dreamt of dwelling in marble halls. So, the architect built him a villa—complete with a marble hall—on a spectacular plot overlooking the sea. The seaward side of the main living room was made entirely of glass to maximize the view. The glass panels could be opened when the weather allowed, which was only about three hundred and twenty days a year.

After he'd been there a couple of years, he invited Maggie and me out for a holiday. This was before Matt.

When we arrived, we dumped our cases and followed Uncle Chas into the sitting room, which was practically pitch dark. He'd installed a thick blackout curtain right along the glass wall, totally obscuring the view. When I asked him why he said that he'd put it there because the light from outside was reflected on the television screen which meant that he couldn't see it properly.

I thought about telling Kemal this story but decided against it in case he took it the wrong way.

We sat back with our drinks—which were wonderful—and looked at the view. The hills on the other side of the valley were turning blue and the sunset was making an inordinate amount of fuss. Why is it that the sun never seems to have grasped the concept that less can be more? We both ignored it.

Kemal wanted to talk politics and I was happy to let him, even though what I know about Turkish politics could easily fit the white spaces on a 10TL note. And besides, I'm not really a putting-the-world-to-rights sort of bloke. Turns out that his politics are liberal and secular and that he is worried about his country. He said that Turkey felt rejected and unwanted by The European Community and that, as a consequence, it was increasingly identifying with Arab states. He said that all this talk of a New Ottoman Empire made him nervous.

He refilled our drinks and we continued to ignore the snacks. The sun was still going through its pathetic attention seeking routine, so we continued to give it the cold shoulder as well.

Kemal then turned his attention to the Turkish education system, which was a small price to pay for the fact that he refilled my drink. More gin than tonic. Perfect. Turns out that Seyhan was a teacher—she's retired now. What followed was a short (but not all that short) monologue on the importance of education for Turkey's young people, which covered all stages from apprenticeships to post-doctoral research fellowships. I had nothing to contribute but it was pretty clear that that was exactly what was expected of me. Apparently, Seyhan used to be a classics teacher and Kemal said that he secretly thought that was a bit of a luxury in a country that needed engineers and computer scientists and biochemists. He asked me not to quote him. I promised that I wouldn't tell anyone apart from Seyhan. So that was all right.

And then he poured us another drink.

By now, the sun had stopped showing off and, realising that no one was taking any notice, had gone off in a huff.

We sat in thoughtful silence for a while and then Kemal asked me if I'd like to see his library. I said that I would and he said perhaps one more drink first and I said why not?

The house was smaller than I expected. It was one of those places where there were knick-knacks and odds and ends on every surface. That would drive me mental. The sitting room and kitchen were open plan and comfortable in a scruffy sort of a way. Beautiful antique cushions were scattered everywhere.

The books were in a kind of lobby between the living area and the bedrooms. I'd been expecting expensively bound volumes of Turkish history, literature and love poetry, but what I found were neat rows of pristine paperbacks by Wilbur Smith, Lee Child, Chris Ryan and—oddly enough—Agatha Christie.

Kemal said that he admired all four writers enormously and that reading their books was an excellent way to keep his English up to scratch. It turned out that he was a particular fan of Agatha Christie and had all eighty two of her detective novels. He said that he thought she wrote 'perfect' prose; 'clear, unambiguous, rhythmic and to the point'. He particularly admired the ones featuring Hercule Poirot (who has always struck me as incredibly irritating) and asked me whether or not I shared this enthusiasm. I had to confess that I hadn't read anything by her since I was a teenager—"Too much sex in them." He ignored this, selected one of the books from the shelf and handed it to me. "Read this and then come back and tell me she is not a genius." I promised that I would.

After this, it seemed logical that we should go back into the living room and that Kemal should pour us both another drink before we flopped down on cushions. But as soon as he sat down he bounced up again and went over to the sideboard. He opened a draw and pulled out a black and white photograph.

"This is my father," he said, as though in answer to a question that I'm pretty sure I hadn't asked. "It was taken in Istanbul in 1938 when he was eighteen. He was training to be an accountant."

The picture was of a skinny, large eyed young bloke with very shiny hair and an eager look on his face. He was wearing a suit that was too big for him and spats. His life was worlds and lifetimes away.

"He was very handsome," I said, for want of anything else to say. When I looked at Kemal, I saw that there were tears in his eyes.

But he soon pulled himself together and did the only thing possible in the circumstances: he poured us another drink, which was a really good idea. And then another, which may not have been such a good idea.

Eventually, I said I ought to go. We shook hands. He offered me a torch but I assured him I wouldn't need it. However, as soon as he shut the door behind me I discovered that that was the wrong answer. For some reason, the garden path was difficult to negotiate in the dark. At one point I stopped and looked upwards. Big mistake. The stars were behaving in ways they're not meant to.

The wooden door in the wall didn't work as well in the dark as it had in the light but in the end I persuaded it to open. I stepped through and closed it behind me without too much of a crash. I steadied myself and that's when I saw the mermaid.

The pool lights were streaming up into the sky, meeting the moonlight that was streaming down on the pool. And splashing around in the middle of it all was a water sprite, an undine, a siren, a naiad, a nereid, an Oceanid, my very own Calypso. Silver and shining and beautiful in the dazzle. I stood there transfixed for what seemed quite a long time.

Then she saw me and smiled. "Did you have a good time?"

Amazing that a mermaid would speak English. My heart was so full that for a moment or two I couldn't think of a reply.

Then the mermaid gave utterance once more: "Can you possibly be as pissed as you look?"

Dark mysteries and kite surfing

D ad has been a bit quiet all day. Just groans from time to time. He obviously has a massive hangover and for some reason Mum seems to find it funny. Every time she looks at him she bursts out laughing.

After breakfast—at which he ate nothing—he said he was going for a dip in the pool. Instead of jumping in or climbing down the ladder, he lay on the side, groaned a bit more and then half rolled, half fell in.

He stayed underwater for a quite a long time, lying on the bottom, as though he was asleep.

When he surfaced, Mum asked, "Feeling better?"

He was as white as a sheet and looked as though he was in pain and said, "No." His hair was in his eyes.

Mum laughed some more.

Very slowly he pulled himself out of the water and staggered across to the hammock where he lay for several hours reading an Agatha Christie novel.

Occasionally, Mum would say something like, "Fancy a beer?" or "A glass of wine?" There was no reply from the hammock.

I have to admit that I thought it was quite funny, but hanging around the pool all day is boring. I thought of going back to the garden to see if Ali was there, but something stopped me. The memory of the look on his face as he fell from the cliff is too fresh.

So I lay on Dad's sun lounger and tried to outstare the grey cat which spent all morning flirting with Mum.

It wandered over to look at Dad in the hammock but he shouted at it to go away. It stared at him for a moment and then ambled back over to us before climbing onto Mum's lounger and curling himself up against her leg.

It didn't go to sleep, though. Its eyes remained open and fixed on my face, when it wasn't sneering at Dad. It was as though it was thinking, weighing things up. Things like how to get rid of us and have Mum to itself. Things like it wouldn't matter that much to it if we were dead. Things like it would happily trade us and all the things we had ever done and ever known, as well as all the things we would ever do and know in the future, for a bowl of biscuits (roast chicken flavour).

Oddly enough, Dad didn't have any lunch, although Mum kindly asked him if he fancied any pickled gherkins, hard-boiled eggs or chilli peppers. No response from the hammock, other than the occasional sigh and muffled snore.

But as the hours passed we could sense that he was beginning to feel a bit better. Not yet anything like a normal human being, but a bit better.

Around two thirty he got out of the hammock with a lot of groaning and moaning and wandered to the pool where he did that falling in and lying on the bottom thing again. When he climbed out, he didn't say anything or even look at us. He just wandered back to his tree, picked up his book and climbed into the hammock with a lot more groaning and moaning.

He was really too big for it; his bum was nearly touching the ground and his feet were above his head. Still, in a funny kind of a way, he seemed happy or as happy as someone who felt as terrible as him could feel.

Mum said that she was sure that the view alone ought to make anyone feel better.

Eventually, Dad rolled out of the hammock and stayed on his feet.

He came over and clapped his hands right by the cat's head. "Pssshhh." It nearly jumped out of its skin then shot up the stairs to the road and disappeared.

"Did you know that Agatha Christie thought that each and every one of us is a dark mystery?"

"Fascinating."

"I'll bet you thought she wrote page-turning detective novels. Well, let me tell you that *Lord Edgware Dies* is an existential *cri de coeur*. Nothing less than an attempt to unravel, the 'maze of conflicting passions and desires' at the heart of each of us. It might even be a Freudian allegory."

"Crikey."

"I know."

"You feeling better?"

"Marginally."

"Fancy a large whisky?"

"Not really."

"Sure?"

"Yep."

"A glass of wine?"

"Not just now."

"A pickled onion?"

"No thanks."

What Dad said he wanted was a trip to the beach, 'to blow the cobwebs away'.

For a change, Mum drove. As we wound slowly down the hill, I could tell that Dad was still thinking about Lord Edgware's death. Only that could possibly explain all the groaning he did.

We drove past the broken door to the garden but there was no sign of Ali. As far as I could see, the place was deserted. It looked peaceful and beautiful in the late afternoon sun.

Dad said he couldn't face the public beach so why didn't we try a little way up the coast?

This meant picking up the main road north. The traffic was terrible, trucks and cars hurtling past without a break.

Mum was driving slowly because she was looking for a turnoff on the right, so almost every car that went past honked at us.

Dad put his hands over his ears and sunk further down in his seat.

Even though we were travelling pretty slowly, we didn't notice the handwritten sign—'*plagi*'—until we had gone past it. Mum pulled over onto the hard shoulder and stopped.

"How the hell are we supposed to turn there if we can't see the sign until the last minute?"

Dad said, "I think I may have commented on the inadequacy of Turkish road signs previously. You might remember. I may have been a tad critical."

Mum didn't reply. She put the car into reverse and backed

up the hard shoulder towards the turn-off. The honking grew more urgent. She ignored it.

We turned off the road and onto a rough track. It was baking hot and in the wing mirror I could see a cloud of dust unwinding behind us as we crawled along, like smoke from a ship's funnel. The only way to avoid driving into the larger holes was to drive into the slightly smaller ones. The car rocked from side to side like a small boat on a rough sea. Dad groaned some more.

On our right were perfect orchards of orange and cherry trees, laid out in neat rows with irrigation channels dug in the red earth. In one orchard, a couple of men were doing something which may have been weeding or may have been just sitting around.

On our left was a seemingly endless chain link fence with three rows of barbed wire at the top. It wasn't clear what the fence was keeping out or keeping in; all we could see on the other side were some scrubby, abandoned-looking fields. Maybe the barbed wire had been put there for birds to perch on, because that was what they were doing—in large numbers. There were gangs of swallows shifting slightly backwards and forwards in order to keep their balance in the breeze and whispering to one another, and loads of larger pale brown birds with crests sticking up from the backs of their heads.

We rocked and swayed along the path for quite a long time, with Dad making an 'aaarrrghh' sound every time Mum failed to avoid a particularly large hole and Mum telling him to man up.

Dad said, "There will never be an end to this road. We are obviously doomed to go on bouncing down it for eternity. It's like being trapped in some kind of mad Greek myth."

We ignored him.

After what seemed like a very long time, the dirt track turned into a tarmac track—not much of an improvement but a bit. And then we came to another of those toll booths in the middle of the road. Just like one at the beach the other day there was no one in it and the barrier was down on one side of the road. So, just as Dad had the other day, Mum drove on—on the wrong side of the road.

In front of us was a huge bay, with the mountains to one side, their slopes dotted with villas, and to our left was an area of marshland with reed beds coming right down to the beach. Behind the reeds there was a double row of tall trees with brown and white mottled trunks and grey green leaves. The branches were lashing from side to side.

When Dad opened his door it almost blew shut again, the wind was so strong.

The beach had been taken over by kite surfers. There must have been seventy or eighty of them, whizzing up and down the water's edge. You could hear the multi-coloured kites snapping and popping in the wind. The riders on the surfboards below were hauling on the lines and being driven up and down the beach at speed. Somehow, although they passed close to each other, they managed not to collide or get their lines tangled. Most of the surfers were men, although there were one or two women. There were, however, a lot of women on the beach, watching and waiting for their blokes.

On the beach itself were a few cafés and places where you could hire kites and boards and wetsuits. They were blasting out songs that Mum and Dad seemed to recognise. Large metal staples had been driven into the sand, and several kites were tied to them. There were quite a few cool-looking dudes with bleached hair and deep tans standing around in groups as though there was nowhere else they'd rather be. They all had bare feet. Dad said that it looked like California.

A gorgeous woman of about twenty walked past us and towards one of the cafes. For no obvious reason she suddenly lifted her T shirt over her head. Underneath she was very brown and very fit. She was wearing a small black bikini. She took no notice of anyone and continued up the beach.

Mum said, "I saw you looking," and I started to go red. But then I realized that she was talking to Dad. She said, "I swear your eyes were out on stalks."

Dad said, "Why would I bother looking at that lithe, tanned, perfect, twenty year-old body when I've got you?"

She punched his arm. Quite hard.

Dad said he was going to go for a swim, but Mum and I didn't want to. He climbed back to the car to get changed (not an easy thing to do) and then started walking into the sea. After about five minutes he was up to his ankles and after another five, he was... up to his ankles. A further five minutes later we could see this distant figure with the water somewhere between his ankles and his knees.

And still he kept plodding forwards towards the sun, which was beginning to set. By now we could only just see him, but the water still didn't seem to be any higher. The wind was blowing sand along the beach so we had to keep our eyes down. Every time we looked up we could see this tiny figure standing still as if waiting for the water to rise until it was deep enough to swim in.

The kite surfers shot up and down, each in his or her own world of waves, wind and speed, taking care not to seem interested in each other or in anyone else.

But no matter how long Dad stood there, the water was obviously not going to rise above his knees. In the end he must have given up because we saw him turn and start plodding back towards us. He kept walking and walking but didn't seem to be getting any closer. After a bit more of this, it began to seem as if he might be right about us being trapped in a Greek myth.

Anyway, he did eventually make it make to shore. "Well," he said, "that was really refreshing. No danger of drowning here. Although a serious danger of being outcooled by just about everyone else."

Mum said, "I thought you looked extremely cool waiting for something to happen with the sea midway up your calves and the sun beating down on you and everyone pretending you weren't there."

Once Dad had got changed in the car (an even more difficult thing to do when you are wet), we wandered down the beach towards the reeds. There was a tiny café with a couple of dudes sitting at a rough wooden table drinking beer, smoking and not talking to each other.

There was a small jetty which stuck out into a channel with reeds on either side. The water was very clear and we could see clouds of tiny silver fish, darting and winking in the sunlight. Swallows were zipping around and masses of blue insects were bouncing up and down. They looked a bit like butterflies and a bit like dragonflies. And they looked as if they were in

137

permanent danger of falling into the water and had to work really hard to stay in the air.

We could see three kites—two red, one bright green—zigzagging among the reeds, as though there was no one attached to them. They seemed to be coming our way and eventually three guys emerged into the channel, leaning back on their boards and tugging the ropes in a very cool manner. They tacked against the wind towards the jetty. They climbed out and let their kites flop down onto the water. They sat on the jetty with their feet in the water, not talking to each other and looking straight ahead at something only they could see. It's hardly worth mentioning that they took no notice whatsoever of us.

As we were walking back down the beach towards the car, Dad said, "The thing about being cool is that you have to pretend not to be able to see things that are right in front of your face. It must be a bit of a strain."

Mum said, "You are well cool enough for me."

Tssit

This morning I visited the garden again.

Everything was still and silent. It was obvious that Ali wasn't there and it felt lonelier and more beautiful than ever without him.

There were no new holes, so he hadn't done any more digging since we last met. I checked the one we'd been working on the other day, but it had started falling in on itself, the earth was trickling down the sides. I picked out a handful of sandy soil. I could feel the force of the past but it was just a tickle compared with the power of the objects in Ali's wooden box.

I wanted to make sense of Ali and my meetings with him.

It was obvious to me that he was dead, a ghost. But that was clearly stupid. As everyone knows, there are no such things as ghosts. And yet that was what he was. *Is.*

I had seen him die. Seen him fall. Been unable to save him. And at the time, I had known—without knowing how I knew—that there was nothing I could possibly do to save him. Ever.

And more than this, it was obvious that he had some sort of mysterious connection with this place and its past. When I was with him I could feel the force and pressure of all that history.

And, just as it seemed to have taken him over, so it seemed to be threatening to take me over as well. It was a scary thought but it was also an exciting one.

And then there was the question of whether or not he knew that he was dead. In many ways he seemed so ordinary, so like everyone else. A bit old fashioned, it's true. A bit serious. A bit shy. And he did seem to know an awful lot about the archaeology of the area and could speak a dead language that he said hardly anyone else knew. But he'd talked about parents and schools and friends. And he'd been really brave about climbing down the cliff and encouraged me to do it, which I never would have done that first time if he hadn't been there to tell me it was OK.

In the end, I came to the conclusion that he probably didn't know. Maybe ghosts never do. Maybe if ghosts did know about their own deaths there is no way they would have the courage to enter the world of the living.

But if he didn't know, how should I respond to him? Should I go along with him and pretend not to know as well? If I was right, telling him what I thought would be far too cruel. I might be triggering something that I could not control. The knowledge might destroy him, if it's possible to destroy a ghost.

A shadow passed across me and I shivered. The sun had been swallowed by clouds that were building up from over the sea. Some bird or other was singing a single, urgent note from the top of one of the trees—Tssit. Tssit. Tssit. I couldn't see it but it sounded like it was trying to say something important. Something I ought to know.

Maybe that something was that the best thing would be to not come here again. Not to see Ali again, and then I wouldn't have to make a decision. But, even so, I knew that I wouldn't be able to stay away.

Why? Because I felt that Ali wanted to be with someone, to be friends with someone. Because I was curious. How many times in my life was I going to come across a ghost? Because I had this feeling that I might be able to learn something from him, something that I wouldn't be able to learn from anyone else.

So, decision made. I wanted to see Ali again and maybe I'd be able to work out how to react to him once I was with him. The problem was that I didn't know where he was. If he wasn't here the only other place that I had seen him was at the cliff. I supposed I'd go and have a look but, at the same time, I told myself that I definitely would not be climbing down to the rock tomb.

When I stood up, I had all these floaters in front of my eyes. I hate that.

The invisible bird was continuing to sing: Tssit. Tssit. Tssit. But now that I'd decided to look for Ali, it sounded more like a welcome. Maybe it was saying, "You. Tssit. Are. Tssit. Safe. Tssit. Here. Tssit. In. Tssit. This. Tssit. Gar. Tssit. Den."

As I ducked my head to climb through the broken door, I could sense someone on the other side standing on the road. For a moment I thought it might be the owner and that I might have to explain myself, but then I realized it was Ali. It was a relief that it was a relief. I was actually happier to see a ghost than a real person.

In that moment, the meeting that I'd been half looking forward to and half dreading suddenly seemed ordinary, not at all spooky.

Ali didn't look like a ghost and didn't act like one, and when

141

he spoke I almost forgot that he was one.

"Hello. Are you here for meeting me?"

I said that I was.

Now that the sky had clouded over it was impossible to check whether or not he had a shadow. And, anyway, what did it matter?

"Shall we go back in again?"

"Sure."

We spent the next couple of hours digging and chatting. And although we didn't find anything, the truth was that, alive or dead, I liked being with him. Even though I'd only met him a couple of times, I felt that he was my friend.

While we were digging, a few drops of rain made dark patches in the dust, but they didn't come to anything.

The lightning was flickering in the sky behind the mountains. Thunder was growling far away. And still the rain didn't come.

Eventually, Ali said that he had to go, that he was having supper with his father, who was finishing work early for the day and would be working on a scholarly paper on the links between the Lycian and Hittite languages (as if I know who the Hittites were). A paper that he would deliver to an archaeological society back in Istanbul.

I said that I would walk home with him. I wasn't sure how he would react to this, but he seemed pleased. He decided not to take his tools with him, but to hide them under a bush, ready for next time.

We walked up the hill together and I wondered what would happen if we met someone and they had heard me talking to Ali. Would they be able to see him and think everything was normal?

Or would they think I was talking to myself?

When we passed our villa I looked over the wall and down the stairs. I could see Mum and Dad lying by the pool. I thought about calling down to them so that I could test whether or not anyone else was able to see Ali. But something stopped me. That would be treating him like a freak. Putting him on display for others. I didn't think it was the way a friend would behave.

It was very humid as we walked along the road, the dust was sticking to my legs and I could feel the sharp edges of the stones through the soles of my shoes.

Once we had left the villa behind, I realized where we were going—the little group of ruined houses that I visited a few days ago with Mum and Dad.

The brushwood barrier was still there, but Ali took no notice of it and sort of walked through it. It's very hard to describe; one minute he was on the same side of the barrier as me, the next minute he was on the other side. He turned round and gestured to me to follow.

I have to admit I hesitated a bit. Following him suddenly seemed like a big deal. It was like having to cross a barrier between two worlds. On this side everything was normal. I could hear distant traffic, Mum and Dad were sunbathing and probably arguing about books nearby, there was a vapour trail in the sky. On this side, everything was predictable, everything followed rules. But who knows what happened on the other side?

But I hadn't come this far to wimp out now. So I tried to walk through the barrier like I'd just seen Ali do. I don't know what I was thinking of and, of course, it shouldn't have worked.

But it did. It worked like this: I walked directly at the barrier, felt a tingling sensation in my legs and there I was on the other side.

Ali smiled.

We walked through the olive trees to where I knew the ruined houses were, although I guessed Ali was expecting to find something else. It was gloomy and cool under the trees. Gnats were dancing in the air.

And then things got *really* weird.

I suppose I'd imagined that Ali would realize that the houses weren't here anymore. That everyone, including his father was long gone. I suppose I'd imagined that he would come face-to-face with reality, even if I wasn't sure how he'd deal with it. But it seemed that when we crossed the barrier we'd left everything familiar behind. Things were different on this side of the brushwood barrier. Very different.

Anyway, it was obvious that Ali wasn't seeing what I was seeing. He wasn't going, "Oh God, what's happened? Where is everyone? What's happened to the houses?" So I guess he was seeing what he expected to see.

I tried to see the village through his eyes.

In the time of Ali and his father, the houses would have been intact and well cared for. The shutters painted. The roofs neatly tiled. The gardens full of flowers and fruit trees. Smoke would be curling out of a couple of the chimneys. The smell of cooking drifting through open windows. Goats would have been tied to the trees. A skinny yellow dog might have been lying sighing with his eyes closed in the dust. Maybe a bonfire would be smoking in one of the gardens. Maybe, a couple of old women would be sitting in the last of the sunshine, embroidering something. They would have watched me and Ali walking towards them. They might have sucked their teeth with disapproval—"Young people these days, no respect. Don't know the meaning of hard work. No sense of responsibility." We might have stopped to wish them a good evening.

Then we might have gone towards one of the houses. We might have crept up to one of the windows and looked in. We might have seen a man sitting at a desk in a pool of light. He would be bent over an old book. There would be other books and papers on the desk. This would be Ali's father, the scholar. He would have a thin face with a hooked nose. He would look like Ali. The same stillness. The same seriousness. If he looked up he would see two faces at his window. For a second he might wonder who we were but then he would realize.

And I guess Ali really did see something like this because he said, "This is my home, will you enter? Can you please remember to step with your right foot first?" He stepped over the doorstep of a ruined house.

And then he disappeared.

That's all I can say.

He wasn't there.

Exactly as if he'd gone into the house and there was a wall between me and him.

The big question was whether or not I should try to follow him and what would happen if I did? The answer was: nothing. I stepped over the doorstep and nothing changed. I was standing inside four ruined walls with the sky above me and the grass beneath my feet. And it was the same everywhere I looked. No sign of Ali.

I sat for a while and waited, but still nothing happened.

I felt very sad and tired and decided it was time to go back to the villa. Back to Mum and Dad.

It was starting to rain when I left. There were slices of cloud in the sky—like the layers in a cake—crossing from one horizon to another. When I got to the brushwood barrier, I tried that walking through it thing again, only this time it didn't work.

I got scratched for my trouble. I watched a thin trickle of blood crawl down my leg. It was as though having let me in, it was now trying to keep me in. In the end I climbed over it. The magic obviously only works in one direction.

Even though I hadn't felt particularly scared when Ali disappeared, I was really pleased to see Mum and Dad when I got back. It was great that they seemed so normal and so familiar.

They had been talking about the piece of rock that I'd left on the windowsill. Mum said that she hadn't noticed it before. Dad said that maybe Elif had picked it up somewhere and thought it'd make a good ornament. It was clear that he wasn't very interested either way. I decided it was best to say nothing. The last thing I wanted was to have to give it back.

Dawn

I t's dawn.

Mist is obscuring the valley floor. The village and the road have disappeared. There's no breeze, but the mist is a shape changer. It boils and shifts and rolls and wafts. Wisps break off and disappear, drifting skywards as the air warms.

The nightingales have just ceased to sing. They will sing throughout the brief nights until the mulberries have ripened. Then they will move on, leaving an echoing silence behind. But now they will sleep for a while and rest their voices.

They doze at their posts like tiny divas in their dressing rooms.

A cat, as grey and slippery as a ghost, is asleep by the pool, curled up, dreaming unimaginable dreams of violence and plenty.

Anneke

I woke this morning to the sound of splashing and children laughing. At first I thought I must still be trapped in a dream but I gradually realized that it was really happening. I sat up in bed and could still hear it. Faintly but quite definitely. It's one of those sounds that seems to travel further than you imagine possible.

I looked at my watch: six thirty. Wherever these children were, they were up and about early.

I rolled over and put my arms around Steve and pressed my face against his back. He muttered something that sounded like, "Don't worry, there's an easy way up. Any minute now." He sometimes has the ability to sleep like a block, a stone, a 'worse than senseless thing', as somebody once said.

I poked him in the ribs and he said, "India really is the most charming country in the late afternoon."

So, I knew that he was awake after all. I slapped his shoulder. But he didn't move, just snored hugely. I clearly wasn't going to get any sense out of him.

For weeks, I've been thinking about that story of the young mountaineer who fell into a glacier and was lost. One of the other people in his group—a man who went on to become a famous glaciologist—calculated, given the glacier's speed and rate of melting, when it would give his friend back. He worked

148

out that it would happen on a certain day in forty three years' time. So, on that day he returned to the glacier and there, as he had calculated, just under the ice, was the body of his friend, lost all those years ago but now returned to the surface. The young man was perfectly preserved in the ice in all his youth and beauty but his friend, the glaciologist, was now an old man, wrinkled and stooped.

It's just a stupid story and couldn't and didn't ever really happen. It's one of those urban legends, a variant on the those-who-the-gods-love-die-young theme. But it's really a brain worm and has taken up residence in my head.

So, when I closed my eyes and tried to go to back to sleep I kept seeing two faces, one young and lovely the other old and sad. I didn't like the way this made me feel, so I climbed out of bed, put on one of Steve's T shirts and went out into the garden to see if I could work out where the children were.

The laughter was coming from behind the Basaks' house and I was irresistibly drawn to it. I climbed the stairs at the back of the villa and turned down the road.

There's a house on the corner just before the steepest bit of the hill. It's always looked empty, but today there was a beaten-up white jeep parked at an odd angle on the drive. The side of the house was smothered with bougainvillea so it was difficult to see into the garden where the pool obviously was.

I didn't know what I was doing there and I clearly couldn't just go in, but I found it impossible to turn around and head back. So I sat on the wall and waited to see what would happen. Left it to fate.

There was a child's plastic toy—a pink dog—on the path,

dropped or abandoned. I had to resist the urge to pick it up.

I'd only been there a few minutes when a youngish woman in a one-piece swimming costume and a sarong came round the corner towards the car. She was very beautiful in a theatrical way: great bones, huge eyes, corkscrew red hair, loads of bracelets. If she was surprised to see a half-dressed mad woman with her hair in her eyes and no shoes sitting on her wall at daybreak she didn't show it.

"Hello."

"Hello."

"Have you been there long?" Her English was faintly accented. Dutch? Danish?

"No. I've been out for a walk. An early morning stroll. I like to walk early. And I was just sitting here for a minute to enjoy the view."

She would have been justified in calling the police then and there.

But what she said was, "Would you like to come in for a cup of coffee?"

"You are very kind. That would be lovely."

She led me round the side of the house. I felt like some kind of monster, my bare feet slapping on the concrete.

There were three children in the pool, two little girls and a little boy. I guess their ages ranged from about five to seven or eight. The little girls might have been twins. They were all wearing arm bands and splashing about with an inflatable crocodile.

They saw me and stopped for a moment looking at me in wonder. Then they squeaked hello and I said hello back. All three had enormous blue eyes and yellow hair.

The woman said, "My name is Anneke. We only arrived last night and the kids woke really early and wanted a swim. I hope they are not making too much noise. I hope they didn't wake you."

I told her my name.

"So, Maggie," she said, "why don't you sit here while I get the coffee? The kids should be all right but maybe you could keep an eye on them for me."

I said that I would and she disappeared inside the villa. I sat on a poolside chair and watched the children playing in the water. The sun was already hot. The water looked so blue that it made my eyes hurt.

I pressed my hand against them at exactly the moment Anneke came back with two mugs of coffee. "Are you OK?"

"Yes, I'm fine thank you."

I felt such a fool. What on earth was I doing there? She must have thought that I was some kind of batty old stalker.

But maybe she was used to waifs and strays because none of this seemed to phase her. Quite the opposite; she seemed glad that I was there. She chatted away as if she had known me forever.

"I am divorced from my husband. I love him but he is a total bastard... This is the first time that the kids and I have been away without him... I know they are going to miss him, but what can I do?... He has a new girlfriend... Our plane was delayed, and when we landed at the airport, all the car hire places were shut. There was no one around. They'd all gone home... I thought we would be spending all night at the airport

but one of the travel reps took pity on us and lent us her car...
She was very kind. She will be coming to collect it later today."

She said all this very matter-of-factly, almost as if she was
telling a story about someone she hardly knew. She didn't seem
to think it was strange saying these things to a complete
stranger.

I wasn't sure how to react. I said something pathetic like,
"Oh, dear." I wasn't surprised that the rep had been kind to her.
There was something about her that seemed to invite it. An
innocence. An assumption that things will work out somehow. I
imagined that she had frequent need of the kindness of strangers.

I told her that we were staying just up the hill. That my
husband was called Steve and my son was called Matt. I still felt
the need to explain my sudden, ridiculous appearance there so I
repeated that I had woken early and decided to go for a walk. I
didn't say anything about the effect that her children's dawn
chorus had had on me or why I'd decided to go walking without
any shoes on.

She looked at me closely for a moment and then said, "I was
glad to find you. I hope we can be friends. I think we shall."

I said that I hoped so too. And I really meant it. I was
strongly drawn to this odd person with her crazy hair and her
children and her air of vulnerability.

She asked me how long we'd been here, what the beaches
were like and whether or not there were any restaurants that she
could take the children to.

I answered her as best I could. The truth was that I was
extraordinarily impressed by the fact that she had apparently
brought the kids here on her own. Certainly, there didn't seem

to be any bloke around. I'm not sure that I could have done it.

We finished our coffee and she produced a tin of tobacco and rolled herself a cigarette. As soon as she lit it, I realized that it was weed. After a couple of puffs, she offered it to me. I was going to say no, but somehow I didn't. I pulled on the little joint for the first time in years, and on an empty stomach. My head spun and my ears buzzed. This definitely had the makings of a pretty strange morning.

The kids were calling something out to her and the crocodile seemed to be leaking air.

"They want me to swim with them. Would you mind?"

"Of course not."

She unwound her sarong and leapt into the pool. The kids screamed with delight as she pulled their legs or threw them into the air. I suddenly felt like a grandmother, although I don't think I'm really old enough even to be her mother.

She had one of the children in her arms. He had wound his arms around her neck and was whispering in her ear.

"He is asking if you would like to swim too."

"I would love to, but I didn't bring my costume." I felt a genuine pang of regret.

Anneke whispered something in the child's ear. He wriggled in her arms.

"I would lend you one but we haven't unpacked properly yet."

I loved the idea that one of her costumes would fit me. I'm twice her size. She was so tiny and so pretty that she made me feel huge and clumsy like a 1960s eastern European shot putter with a chin like Desperate Dan, shoulders like a WWF wrestler and ears like a hobbit.

"Why don't you come in anyway? In your T shirt."

And the fact was that I couldn't think of a single reason. Perhaps it was the weed, but I got out of my chair and jumped straight in. It was lovely. I splashed around and dived under the water and gave the kids rides on my back, and screeched and splashed and bobbed up and down with them.

Eventually, we all got cold, climbed out and lay on the edge of the pool in the sunshine, the kids in a pile, Anneke and me side by side. The minute we got out of the water, the swallows came down to drink. It was if they'd been watching us and waiting for their chance.

Anneke made another spliff.

I felt like I never wanted to leave, but I knew that I had to.

Anneke said, "Please come again. Please come any time."

I said that I would and that she must feel that she could come to our villa any time and use our pool.

Then I walked back with Steve's T shirt clinging to me and my hair still dripping. I wasn't sure how I was going to explain all this when I got back. But what I *was* sure about was that I felt great. Happier than I've felt for a very long time.

This is not Ephesus

Today, we finally went on a successful trip to an ancient city, although not the one beginning with 'S', which Ali had told me might have been the first one that the Lycians built after they had arrived from Crete. I didn't think even that fascinating piece of information was likely to make Dad agree to go there again.

The good news was that he seemed fully recovered from his evening with Mr Basak—"It would have been rude to refuse that seventh drink,"—and drove. It was a boiling morning and the main road was packed with traffic. No one was stopping at the orange stalls. The mountains disappeared into the distance on both sides and in front. Green, then dark blue, then pale blue, then hardly there at all, then merging into the sky.

We passed a restaurant and next to it was a field of tall metal poles with circular platforms on top. There were scruffy nests and groups of three or four of what Mum said were storks— adults and chicks—on most of them. These were the birds I'd seen on the chimney in the village.

We crossed a low, metal bridge over a grey-green, slow-moving river that was almost choked with weed. We could hear a roaring noise. Dad stopped the car and we climbed down the river's bank to a rough footpath. We followed this back round a bend in the river and found a waterfall. The banks were so steep and so close together that it was forcing the water to spurt outwards in an arc. The air was full of spray. There were ferns and plants with large glossy leaves everywhere. The water fell into a black pool.

A few kilometres further on, we came to a really busy seaside town. There were loads of shops and restaurants and discos all crammed together in narrow streets clogged with traffic. We drove round and round for ages before we found somewhere to park, and even then we weren't sure that we were parking legally. Dad said he wasn't so much parking as accepting that he just didn't care any longer.

We walked down to the harbour which was directly opposite a huge new police station. Lots of policemen were posing on the front lawn and not doing much of anything in particular.

There were many small boats tied moored in the harbour and as soon as we started looking at them we were surrounded by men trying to persuade us to take theirs.

Dad eventually decided that we should go with a huge man with an enormous black beard. He pointed to himself and said, "Hello."

Mum said, "*Guneydin.*"

He said, "No, my name Hello." He put his thumb to his ear and his little finger to his lips, miming speaking on the telephone.

And as that seemed to be the only English he knew, we had no way of checking that we had understood and had to accept that he knew what he was talking about. It was certainly an easy name to remember.

He had a small single-masted boat with a loose white canopy

running the length of its pale blue hull. Its name—*Yuruk*—was painted on its side in rough black letters.

Hello started the engine, untied the rope that was attached to a bollard on shore and backed slowly out of the tiny harbour.

Once we had cleared the harbour wall, he turned the boat around and pointed her across the bay. The water was choppier out there and the breeze was stronger. The light was dazzling. Mum, Dad and I sat on a small bench towards the back of the boat. Every few minutes, Hello would check that we were OK and smile and wave.

We followed a narrow channel with banks of reeds on either side. Several other small pale blue boats were chugging this way and that. Houseboats were moored to poles that had been sunk into the river bed.

There was a restaurant with a wooden terrace at the front, which was hanging out over the water, and a hotel with its own jetty, on which people were sunbathing.

Beyond the reeds on one side was reddish cliff, with several rock tombs carved out of it. Hello slowed the boat so that Mum could take photographs. He took the opportunity to flick a switch and Turkish disco started blaring out of speakers. Mum looked at Dad and Dad looked at Hello, put his fingers in his ears and slowly shook his head. Hello waved apologies and turned the music off.

A crag of rock towered above us and we could just make out a wall on the top of it. Inside the wall were ruined buildings.

Hello pointed and said, "Citadel." So, he did speak at least one more word of English.

He steered the boat closer to the reeds and we could see that they were full of hundreds of swallows, many of them clinging in groups to a single stem. Mum said she couldn't believe how beautiful everything was and smiled at Hello. He smiled back even though he obviously didn't understand her. Maybe he thought she'd said that she would like to sail away with him or asked him if he liked football or what he wanted for Christmas. He then showed her the time on his watch and smiled. Mum looked confused then shook her head and smiled. He looked concerned and then smiled. Dad and I smiled. Mum, who had been looking in her phrase book, then pointed at where the boat's name was painted and said, "Wanderer." Hello looked confused and then smiled.

Dad said, "I think 'Nomad' is a better name for a boat."

Everyone nodded for a bit as if they were thinking hard about this and then we all smiled again.

This was only brought to an end when Hello cut the engine and pointed to a large bird picking its way through the reeds. Mum said that it was a purple heron. It had a wicked beak and a beautiful crest on the back of its head.

We drifted slowly into an even tinier harbor than the one we'd set off from and Hello moored *The Nomad* against a high wall. Mum and Dad then performed a series of complicated mimes intended to let him know that we would be back in two hours. He smiled, held Mum's hand as we stepped ashore, then lay down on one of the benches, covered his face with his handkerchief and appeared to fall instantly asleep.

A man on an enormous tractor said that he would be delighted to drive us up to the ancient city for the small matter of around 150TL.

Dad said, "You are very kind but we prefer to walk."

The man looked at us as if we were mad. "But it is very hot. This is the hottest part of the day."

Dad said, "Yes, we know. It is our favourite time of day for walking up steep hills."

The man shrugged, turned away and took no further notice of us.

About halfway up the hill, I think Mum and Dad were beginning to wish we had taken him up on what was beginning to seem like a generous offer.

After a hard climb of about ten minutes we came to a wire mesh fence and a pay booth. For a change there *was* someone in the booth. A bored-looking guy in his early twenties, who sold us tickets in perfect English.

Mum asked him if there was a guide book. He made a huge effort to respond to her and said, "There is only this," and held up a faded paperback with the picture of an elaborate two-storey ruin on its cover.

Mum looked at the picture and said, "But isn't that a picture of Ephesus?"

"Yes, it is Ephesus."

"So, is it a guide book to Ephesus?"

"It is."

"And isn't Ephesus nearly two hundred kilometres away?"

"Yes it is."

"So, the book is not very much use to us is it?"

"No, but it is all that there is." He said this as if there was nothing that could be done about it. Nothing. Ever.

"So, would you like to buy it?"

"What do you think?"

"I would think that you do not."

"You are right." When she said this, the guy smiled for the first time.

Then, also for the first time, he said something without any prompting from us: "The people of this place were gravely afflicted by malaria. It is said that the sickness turned them green. It was known as the place where even the dead walk."

For a minute, none of us could think of anything to say to this and he didn't seem to expect us to.

Then Dad said, "Well, that's something to look forward to. But before we take out chances with the green people, can we get some coffee or a beer or something?"

The smile faded. "There are only crisps. Sour cream flavour."

"So, not exactly the perfect snack when you are as thirsty as we are."

"No, not really. There is a water tap in the toilet. You can drink from that if you like."

"Sounds delicious."

After so much conversation, the bloke in the booth looked exhausted. We left him there and didn't take up his offer of a refreshing drink in the bogs.

We walked under a kind of awning and emerged into the incredible heat of the lunchtime sun. We were standing in a large open area with a dirt floor. There wasn't any shade apart from a small patch under a couple of olive trees, so we scuttled over to the smaller one and cringed underneath it as if our lives depended on it.

When we had recovered a bit, we scuttled over to the larger

one and found a couple of other people already sitting under it. From here, we could see down into a huge amphitheatre; row upon row of seats carved out of the rock. The heat was like being hit over the head. The cheap seats were much narrower and closer together than the expensive ones, a few of which had names carved on them. Dad said that they must have been used for the Lycian equivalent of corporate hospitality.

Parts of the amphitheatre were collapsed as if they'd suffered earthquakes. There were lots of large black and yellow butterflies flitting around and little blue grey birds which Mum said were nuthatches.

When we reached the area where the stage area would have been, Dad stretched his arms wide and started singing in Italian. Mum and I ran and hid in the shade of another tree in case anyone thought we were with him.

We needn't have worried because it seemed that the only other people here were those two hiding under the second tree, and they hadn't moved. Perhaps they were asleep. Perhaps they were trying to swallow sour cream-flavoured crisps. Perhaps they were trying to work out how their Ephesus guide book related to this place.

Beyond the amphitheatre, there was a slippery pavement that ran steeply downhill. The dark grey stones had been polished to a glassy sheen by thousands of years of people walking on them. The pavement had some of the electrical force that everything old around here seems to have. It made my feet tingle, like pins and needles. Long pale grasses were poking up between the stones. Cicadas were squawking from every crack in the rocks. Lizards were darting about and we even saw a rat.

The pavement led past a temple, which was nothing more than two rows of columns, all of which looked as though they'd been snapped off by some angry giant. I remembered what Ali had said about people nicking all the stone they could get away with to build their own houses and barns. There must be some pretty posh barns in the area.

There wasn't much information on the signs so we didn't really know what we were looking at. One pile of stones was described as a Roman baths. It had three huge arches with a fantastic view over the sea but no obvious baths, although there were a couple of brick-lined channels that might have been used to pipe hot water. Or they might have been used for some other purpose entirely.

As we walked downhill we came to a flat shady area which, the sign said, had once been the site of a sacred fountain. The sacred fountain was represented by a smaller pile of rubble than the Roman baths, so it was kind of hard to visualize. But it had atmosphere and it was possible to imagine people walking here, talking philosophy or picnicking under the trees thousands of years ago. Today, it was peaceful and beautiful and full of grazing cows with bells round their necks. The cows were sweet and inquisitive, smelt delicious and rubbed their soft noses against Mum's hand.

When we walked to the far edge of the flat area, the land fell away again, and beyond that we could see what had once been the harbour but was now choked with reeds. It was obvious that once the sea had started receding this place wouldn't have been much use as a port. Several small boats were winding along the zigzag channel to the sea.

This was as far as we went.

We turned back and trudged up the hill to the entrance.

As we went through the turnstile, Dad said to the bloke in the booth, "Have you sold many of those Ephesus guide books today?"

"Not many."

"Have you sold any?"

"Not really."

"How about those sour cream crisps?"

"Not many."

"Any?"

"No, unfortunately not."

"Maybe you need to reconsider your stock policy."

The guy in the booth smiled a secret smile and waved to us as we set off down the hill to rejoin Hello.

"Perhaps we will have a new guide book next year."

Dad called back, "Make sure you hang onto one for me. How about a new flavour of crisps?"

"Maybe so."

Hello sat up as soon as we approached the boat and produced bottles of cold water from a little fridge in a cupboard in the middle of the deck. He smiled a lot which Mum interpreted as his way of asking us if we had enjoyed the ruins. Mum, who seemed to have given up on the hope of being understood, said that she had found the place very 'moving', which would have puzzled Hello even if he had understood the word. This was followed by a bit more smiling before we set off again.

We wound in and out of reedy channels, sometimes heading directly towards the sea, sometimes directly away from it. We waved to the people in other boats and to a couple of guys fishing in waders. A large bird, which Mum said was a marsh harrier, flew over. Hello pointed to it as proudly as if he had hand reared it and trained it to be in precisely that spot at precisely that moment.

We crossed a small lagoon and headed for a stone jetty which had dozens of boats moored to it. Somehow Hello managed to squeeze *The Nomad* into a non-existent space between two larger boats.

He killed the engine and went straight back to sleep. We climbed onto the harbour wall, where a guy wearing a military uniform sold us tickets to the beach. There were hundreds of people here, most of them in swimming costumes. Ticket guy told us that the beach was a Special Environmental Protection Area because of the loggerhead turtles that had been laying their eggs on this strip of beach for hundreds, perhaps thousands, of years. Because they lay at night, no one was allowed on the beach after dark.

Mum pointed to a new building on the sand and said, "But isn't that a hotel?"

Ticket guy explained that about thirty years ago a development company had built a hotel here without the necessary permissions. In the end, the local council made it illegal for them to go on building. This was seen at the time as a great victory for conservation. But it's not yet a total victory because although the development company was ordered to demolish the hotel they haven't done so and have been fighting the decision in the courts ever since. So, for the moment, the building still stands. Empty and never used.

The beach was enormous. To the right were a couple of wooden cafes with palm trees and across the bay to the left a pine forest stretched right to the shore.

The sun was thumping down and ricocheting off the sea, so we hired sunbeds and umbrellas and lay there for quite a long time as though we had been knocked out.

All along the beach were metal pyramids about a metre high. Signs on them explained that they were there to mark the presence of turtle eggs under the sand and were not to be disturbed.

Next to us was a group of Turkish women in full-length swimming costumes—ankle to neck—and headscarves, wearing loads of jewellery. Every few minutes a couple of others wandered up from somewhere to join them. Within an hour, there must have been thirty of them, talking, laughing, smoking and eating lots of fruit. Only two of them were not fully covered: one was wearing a one-piece gold costume and the other a scarlet bikini. This didn't seem to strike any of them as odd. Mum smiled at them and they smiled back at her.

The sea was the colour of brass, the glare hurt my eyes. A disturbance in the water caught my attention and then a humped back broke the surface with hardly a ripple. A head lifted out of the water, like the periscope on a submarine. It was a turtle swimming towards the shore. Maybe her need to lay eggs was so urgent that she couldn't wait until sunset. For a second my eyes locked with hers which were moist and reflected the light. She looked very ancient and wise. But in that short time, she must have seen enough. The beach was obviously out of the question. So she turned and headed back out to sea, tucked her head in and dived. I couldn't see her any more.

Eventually, it was time to go and we walked back over the sand to the harbour. Hello jumped to attention as soon as he heard us. More smiling and nodding followed. Having wedged us in between two larger boats, getting us out was a bit of a problem. He revved the engine, put us into reverse and pushed as hard as he could against the hulls on either side and we shot out into open water like a cork coming out of a bottle. Diesel fumes drifted across the harbour.

As Hello turned *The Nomad* around, I looked back the way we had come. The sun was low in the sky and was shining through the unglassed windows and empty rooms of the unfinished hotel. I wondered if it would ever be finished or would it still be here two thousand years from now, an ancient monument like the citadel and the amphitheatre?

Maybe tourists at some distant point in the future would come down from the citadel and wander its ruined shell, trying to imagine what life was like back when it was built, wondering what kind of people we were. Maybe they would think it was some kind of a shrine to the turtles we obviously worshipped.

The voyage back took an hour and was magical. The sun was setting over the sea. The light was soft and pale. Mum sat back on her bench and trailed her hand in the water. The water in the channels was silent and oily, the reeds moved just ever so slightly. Behind us we could see about twenty other boats all heading the same way as us. Each of them had a large headlight mounted on the bow. Beams of light caught the reeds and bounced off the water. Ahead there were just a couple of other boats, their wakes spreading slowly towards us. We could see groups of shadowy figures on some of the other boats. There must have been a couple of hundred of people in total. All going the same way. All silent and peaceful and amazed.

The lights of the town and the water-side hotels winked red, green and gold in the dusk and were reflected in coloured scribbles on the black water. We could hear the voices of people sitting in restaurant gardens, quiet laughter, the clink of cutlery, glasses touching glasses.

A couple of late swallows flew to their nest in the reeds. The moon rose over the citadel. An owl drifted silently overhead.

The three of us were in a kind of trance. We didn't want the journey to end. If this was all the future held, then that would have been fine with us. At that moment, it would have seemed greedy to ask for more.

Finally, Hello tied up in the harbour where we had first met him. He helped Mum ashore while she said '*tesekkur ederim*' about a hundred times. Hello smiled and bowed. Before Dad went on shore he handed him quite a large pile of Turkish notes. I swear there were tears in Hello's eyes. He said thank you about a hundred times, with his hand on his heart. Then he hugged Dad and to my amazement Dad hugged him back. It was really embarrassing and kind of nice at the same time.

Twenty six things about Maggie's nbf

Maggie's got a newbie, an nbf.

The first I knew that she'd gone walkabout the other morning was when I was sitting outside necking a leisurely cup of coffee and she came slopping and splashing down the stairs from the road. She was soaked through and her hair was dripping. She looked like she was freshly arrived from the bottom of the ocean. Maybe she really is turning into a mermaid. All she needed was a strand of seaweed in her hair and a bra of abalone shells. She was really happy. Talked a storm about this woman she'd met who's staying at the villa on the corner and about her children. How original and lovely she was, how gorgeous and unselfconscious they were. How intrepid she'd been bringing them all here on her own. Said they'd all had an early morning swim. Said this as though it was absolutely normal to dunk yourself in a complete stranger's pool hours before anyone sensible is abroad. And then she added that she had smoked dope with this woman as though that was entirely normal as well. And all before breakfast.

She mentioned Anneke a few more times on the fantastic trip to the ancient city that wasn't Ephesus. Said things like, "She's really amusing and original and brave. You must meet her." I tried to muster the required amount of enthusiasm.

Anyway, this morning she said, "I'm going down to see

Anneke. I'm going to ask her here for a drink and something to eat this evening."

"What about her kids? Where's she going to get a babysitter from?

"She doesn't need one. She can bring them here."

To be honest, I wasn't exactly looking forward to this, but I knew there was no stopping Maggie. If she wanted to adopt this woman and her kids there was nothing I could do about it. And it was great to see her so happy.

"OK. Why not? It'll be fun. In that special sense of the word in which other people's kids are fun, obviously."

At this point, Maggie said something about my enthusiasm levels being critically low. "Any lower and you'll cease to exist altogether. Any lower and there'll just be a wavy line in the air where you once were. A tiny ripple in space and time. A geometric point. A nothingness. A nullity. A cosmic dead end."

OK, OK. So, I put on my enthusiastic face and she said she'd be back in about ten minutes. This time, she'd remembered to wear her swimming costume under her own T shirt. Makes a change.

Two hours later she was back. Said she'd got a bit 'caught up'. I nodded like someone who was interested.

"Anyway, she's coming this evening and she's bringing the children with her. They're called Elsje and Hedy—they're girls, and the boy is Bastiaan. It'll be a chance for us to help her out a bit."

"Marvellous, I'm really looking forward to meeting them." At which point, for some reason, she punched my shoulder.

"They'll be here at eight so we've got lots of shopping to do.

We'll need food and nibbles and lemonades and cokes for the kids. I'll make you a list and perhaps you can drive down to the supermarket for me and get the stuff."

"OK, but aren't you coming?"

"No, I want to spend some time here with Matt. Just the two of us. I don't want him getting jealous of Anneke's kids."

I wasn't happy about this. I thought about insisting that given that she had invited this woman, then she really ought to come shopping with me. But in the end I let her have her own way.

Then she went into a long riff about Anneke. The salient points—in no particular order—were: (1) Anneke lives in Amsterdam and works in the fashion business as some kind of PR; (2) her ex-husband is a well known fashion photographer and a total bastard who doesn't realize what he's lost; (3) that total bastard's new girlfriend is only twenty three—practically young enough to be his daughter; (4) that Anneke once had an audition for a part in quite a famous film but in the end didn't get the role, even though it was clearly made for her; (5) that total bastard has said he wants more children with the twenty three year-old and that his childcare payments are extremely erratic and that he's trying to reclaim some of the furniture that he left behind when he moved out; (6) that Elsje and Hedy are very artistic and sensitive and go to a stage school; (7) that Anneke has a new boyfriend, five years younger than her, who started off well but who is now turning out to be a total bastard as well. He was supposed to be coming on this holiday but cried off at the last moment with some pathetic excuse, leaving Anneke to manage on her own; (8) that the villa belongs to some friends of Anneke's parents who are allowing her to stay there for free; (9) that Anneke makes many of her own clothes and most of her children's and sells hand-made jewellery at boot fairs at weekends; (10) that, total bastard though he was, the first total bastard was apparently a brilliant shag. (How had they got around to discussing that? I can't imagine ever asking Kemal what he and his missus get up to in the sack, however many gins we'd had); (11) that Anneke and one of her mates have set up a support group for their friends—and there are apparently quite a lot of them—whose husbands turned out sooner or later to be total bastards of one kind or another. The club apparently focuses on a combination of relaxation techniques and witchcraft—a blend of mindfulness and black magic; (12) that Anneke has a twin sister who also has three children and whose husband is a bit flakey (a total bastard in the making) but hasn't actually taken up with a twenty three year-old as of yet; (13) that Anneke enjoys her job and is well paid but doesn't feel that she is being challenged intellectually. Once the kids are old enough, she's hoping to go back into full-time education; (14) that Anneke's father is a dentist; (15) that Anneke has been to this part of Turkey a number of times in the past. She and total bastard used to come here before they had kids and she's pretty sure that Elsje and Hedy were conceived here; (16) that the new boyfriend (TBITM) says that he has never met, let alone been with, anyone like Anneke. (She apparently thinks this is a compliment. I think that it might be interpreted in a number of ways); (17) that Anneke thinks she might be gluten intolerant and is trying to cut out dairy products from her diet and that she's finding it very hard to get almond milk around here; (18) that Anneke's star sign is Sagittarius. (Anneke says that

Sagittarians are highly evolved. That they are travelers and metaphysicians for whom the day-to-day world isn't enough. Apparently, they can be a little impractical because they are so focused on the noumenal. However, she also says that she shares many of the attributes of Librans—she has an ideal sense of peace and harmony, even if both states are elusive in her own life. And of those born in Scorpio—she always wants to penetrate below the surface of reality. And a bit of Pisces—she dreams of a life without limitations. It shows how smitten Maggie must be that she is prepared to countenance this load of old bollocks without actually exploding); (19) that Anneke has a cousin—her mother's sister's daughter—who lives in Paris; (20) that Anneke has always felt different from other people and was bullied at school because the other girls were jealous of her; (21) that while she was married to total bastard, Anneke got her revenge for the fact that he was always having affairs by having three affairs of her own, one of which turned out to be more serious than she'd intended. She made sure that total bastard knew about all three, but he didn't seem particularly bothered. In fact, Anneke sometimes felt that he was positively encouraging her; (22) that Anneke doesn't think she wants to have any more children but doesn't believe in birth control and feels that she's too young to be sterilized; (23) that Anneke thinks of herself as a Buddhist, it's just that her life is so full on that she doesn't have time to meditate and, of course, the kids need material things; (24) that Anneke has never voted in any kind of election, local or national; and (25) that Anneke clearly has a gift for friendship, a talent for empathy. She's just so *nice*.

And that's pretty much all I can remember. It seems like

quite a lot given that I've never even met the woman. In fact, it seems so much that I can't figure what I'll get out of actually meeting her that I don't already have.

I may have missed one or two bits but that's more or less the nub of Maggie's gist.

Oh, and I've just remembered one more for luck: (26) that Anneke is thinking about learning to play the cello.

Enargeia

Sitting here, I feel guilty and sad and irritated and claustrophobic and angry and sleepy and bored and a little bit mad and restless and depressed and inadequate and overwhelmed.

It's taken me my whole life to learn that I can feel all these things at the same time.

As she gets older and frailer, Mother looks less and less like a person. More and more like an insect or an animal.

She has lost most of her hair, and her face, which has fallen in on itself (she is refusing to wear her teeth), has become increasingly angular and beaky.

She's like a tortoise or a lizard or a species of monkey the name of which I can't remember. In some lights, there is something extraterrestrial about her. As if she is wearing her skeleton on the outside.

What's left in her bed is what happens to a person once you take away everything that made them a person.

When I was teaching, I used to talk to my students about *enargeia*, which is a particularly fugitive notion and useful as a way of illustrating the problems of reading great literature in translation.

Ancient rhetoricians and critics used it to describe the extraordinary clarity of Homer's prose.

Essentially, the word describes the overwhelming radiance of the gods as they mingle with mortals as themselves rather than disguised as humans.

Translators have struggled for a synonym. But words such as 'vividness' and 'fullness' and 'truth' don't quite capture it. *Enargeia* is scary.

I used to say to my students that *enargeia* refers to things that are as fully themselves as it is possible to be. All other possibilities, all doubts, approximations and compromises trail in its wake.

There is nothing comfortable about gods. When they appear, they are so fully themselves that they create a rift—a kind of interference—in the fabric of reality. They make everything else seem transitory and cursory, evanescent and suspect. They pull the rug out from under us.

Enargeia is the most extraordinary intensity of existence.

And I can see no reason why this concept should be reserved for the deathless gods. It seems to me that it can just as easily be the defining characteristic of certain humans. People who are so fully themselves that they too rip apart the fabric of reality, causing us to revisit our notions of what it means to exist.

We don't have to love, like or admire them, but they sure as hell make us sit up and take notice.

Mother was like this. I knew it even as a child although, of course, I didn't then have the words for it. Certainly she was scary enough. Not because she was physically intimidating, but because she was so certain of herself, so sure of her own rightness, that it would have taken far more courage than I ever had to question or challenge her.

Not that would have mattered much either way. She was pretty much indifferent to whatever I might do or feel. Her sense of herself was so intense that it didn't leave all that much room for a sense of others. Specifically, it didn't leave much room for a sense of me.

In fact, she wasn't really good with other people full stop. Didn't really get them. Although my brothers seemed to find her easier to cope with than I ever did. Not that they've done much coping recently. They've more or less left it to me.

I always felt that she felt that I was nothing more than a pale reflection of her. Which, I guess, was why she always acted as if it was OK to give me orders. "Make me a cup of tea... Brush your hair... Water the garden... Love me and me alone."

And when I was an adult, the orders continued: "Don't wear that frock, it doesn't suit you... I'm coming to stay with you for two weeks... Buy a different brand of coffee... Continue to love me and me alone."

Even when I was in the States, I didn't feel that I was out of reach.

The only time I ever really stood up to her was when she told me that I'd be a fool to marry Kemal. I went ahead and did it anyway. Initially she said that she wouldn't be coming to the wedding. But when I didn't beg her to, she relented and came, radiating chilly disapproval.

I thought at the time that it was a victory for me, that she had capitulated, that a new order had been initiated.

I was wrong, of course. Nothing changed. The fact that I was a married woman made no difference other than suggesting new possibilities for domination: "Always have you husband's supper ready when he comes in from work... Never say no to him in bed... Always look your best for him."

Ironic really, given that she never thought Kemal was good enough for me. Her lust for power was stronger than her sense of his shortcomings.

And now all that certainty, all that conviction about her absolute right to occupy her place in the world, has vanished. A life that was once so full it could scarcely contain itself has dwindled to nothing.

She lies there, sometimes inert, sometimes more agitated. When agitated, she talks incessantly, either to herself or to me, I've never been able to decide. She's telling herself, or me—or the universe at large, I suppose—a story. But it is a story without a beginning or an end. A story without structure. A never-ending commentary on life as she now perceives it, if perceives is the right word. A story built of the wrong words in the wrong order. And sometimes not even words; just the tattered remnants of words. Random, half-remembered syllables dredged up out of unfathomable darkness. Sometimes single letters. Vowels and consonants. Sometimes sounds: 'huh', 'wwhhh', 'blll', 'tat', 'ddrr'.

When you switch the light on in here, the bulb seems to work in reverse. It sucks the light out of the room, leaving a kind of dirty twilight, like the scum round the side of an empty bath. I can hear someone howling down the corridor. Shadows creep past Mother's door on walking frames. Living ghosts.

Mother is supine on a hospital bed with an inflatable mattress to prevent bed sores. She's been like this for three years.

I send money to the manager so that there are always fresh

flowers in here. When I was a child she always had them in the house, even if it meant going without supper for a day or two, even if it meant *her children* going without supper for a day or two.

I say fresh, but for some reason they never look very wonderful, always past their best. I sometimes wonder if he pockets the money I send and brings the flowers from funerals. After all, in his line of business, he goes to enough of them. Not that mother takes any notice of them.

The room contains no trace of her personality. When she was able to express a preference, she would never allow me to personalize the place. I used to suggest that I brought in pictures or a bookcase or one of her cabinets of knick-knacks. But she wouldn't have it. She used to say, "This is not my home and never will be." Rather than importing any comfort or colour (the walls are painted a pale ochre), she was determined that her room should retain its institutional anonymity. By that time it was the only form of protest available to her.

There's a small ornamental tree directly outside in the window. For three years I've thought that I must identify it but I haven't yet done so. I don't really understand what's stopping me. Its branches mark the seasons. Three times now it has produced buds which have swollen to jagged leaves, only to flare scarlet and then die back and drop in the autumn. When Mother first came here, I used to try to draw her attention to it. Made fatuous remarks about the beauty of the light on the leaves or the way the bare branches moved in winter gales. Pointed out the small dark bird with white spectacles on its face that sometimes sits on one of the branches, apparently checking up on us. But I could never capture her interest. Most of the time she turned her face away from the window and towards the wall. I once asked her why she didn't seem to enjoy watching it and she said, "Because it's jeering at me, although I know I can't expect you to believe that."

But the truth is that I *do* know what she means.

I'm holding her hand, which is almost translucent. It's inert in mine. I don't know if she has any idea what I'm doing. And if she does, whether or not she wishes it.

She never was a touchy feely person, even when... I almost thought, "Even when she was alive."

The English woman was right

We've got guests this evening. Mum seems amazingly pleased that Anneke and her children are coming. She's really excited.

All day she's been trying to communicate to Elif that we're going to have visitors. Elif is practically having to hold her down to prevent her from cleaning the kitchen. Any minute now they'll be wrestling over the mop and bucket.

There's no place for me in all this so I decide to visit the garden again.

As usual, Ali's digging when I get there and has already worked up a sweat. He doesn't mention the other evening when I went home with him.

"This is very good place to dig. As if the earth wishes to give up its treasures. As if it pushes them into my hand. Baba says there are many towns and cities on this coast that are forgotten by history or remembered only as names. He says there is no such place as this anywhere else in the world."

He shows me what he has found today: a small brown metal disc which may have been a coin and a comb made out of bone which has lost only a couple of teeth. Somehow I know what it feels like to drag that comb through your hair, precisely how it scrapes across your scalp. That it once smelt of the perfumed oils its owner used to make her hair shine. How can I possibly know this?

I think about what Ali has just said. If his father is right, there could be an entire city under our feet and the things that Ali has dug up are just the tiniest clues about what life there was like. Trying to understand a civilization from the fragments he has found would be like trying to recreate a human being from their toenail clippings. It would be like archaeologists in three thousand years' time thinking they knew something about Dad because they'd dug up the rusted remains of his watch. What could they possibly know about how funny he is and how grumpy he likes to pretend to be?

The people who lived here all those years ago have been swallowed up by the earth, become part of the landscape. That must be why I like to think of the tomb inscription being built into the front wall of the house in the village. It means that the dead are still connected with the living. And maybe it's why it was so important to me to carve my name on the wall of the tomb.

I squat down beside Ali and together we sift through the crumbly earth. I feel that although this garden is full of surprises they will never be bad ones.

After a couple of hours, we strike another of those pieces of grey stone with the egg shapes and the triangles carved on it. It's much bigger than the first piece and it takes some time to work it out of the ground. We clear the dirt from it but it's so big we can hardly lift it.

Obviously we can't take it back with us. Ali says that we should place it at the base of one of the corkscrew trees, as an offering for the gods of this garden. I think he's joking but it doesn't seem such a mad idea. So we walk the piece of carved stone through the grass, end over end, and leave it leaning against the trunk in the shade. As we do so, it scrapes the dark bark of the trunk leaving a small white scar where the heartwood shows through.

We're too tired to go on digging. As the sun sinks in the sky the clouds start to build. The air becomes humid.

And as I knew he would, Ali asks me if I want to come home with him. All this time I've been thinking how to tell him that he's dead, but I can't think of any way that wouldn't break his heart. So, I say nothing.

When we reach the brushwood barrier, Ali walks through it and I follow him without really thinking about it. It's easy once you get the knack of it.

As soon as I go through, I'm aware that things are different from the last time. I can hear the spring running much more strongly, as though after heavy rain, and the ground under the olive trees is tidier, as if someone has raked it. Around several of the orange trees there are circles made of blocks of stone, which weren't there before and which, I guess, are to hold water. And the houses are different in a way that's hard to describe. Whereas before they were low and tumbledown, no higher than my waist, now it's as if an image of a whole house has been placed on top of those ruined foundations. Shimmering roofs and doors and windows. Not quite solid, more like a hologram.

It's quite clear where the real stone ends and the illusion of a house takes over, but together the real and the not real make some kind of whole.

Blurry figures are moving between the houses. Like faded

photographs. There's a faint smell of wood smoke in the air, like a memory that you have to work really hard to recover. A memory of something that happened a long, long time ago.

Just as before, Ali steps up to one of the houses; only this time I don't have to imagine it, I can see exactly how it used to look—small and tidy with neat rows of plants. I follow him into the garden and we stand next to a wooden post that's been driven into the ground—a post that shimmers in and out of existence—and look in through the window.

And just as I imagined it, there's a stooped figure at the desk wearing a velvet cap with a tassel, poring over a book in a circle of light cast by an oil lamp. He holds a magnifying glass in one hand. His face is lined, his nose thin and hooked, his eyes sunk, his skin papery. The cap doesn't entirely cover a bald spot. He looks exhausted. The light from the lamp highlights the creases and folds in his face, the hollows of his eye sockets. A cigarette rolled in black paper is dangling from his lips.

Ali is close to tears, "But I do not understand. He is so old. What has happened?"

I think I know but I can't think how to say it.

And just as I knew he would, the old man looks up and sees our faces at the window. His eyes look so tired and for a moment it's as though he doesn't know what he's looking at. Maybe his attention is still on the ancient world he's been studying for so long. Perhaps he's seeing crowds of people moving about in a market square three thousand years ago, or a priestess with a golden circlet round her wild hair receiving an offering of honey and figs from a visitor to the shrine she guards. But then he drags himself back to the present. His eyes focus on us and he smiles. He gets slowly to his feet and walks to the window as if to see us better. Then he gestures us into the house.

Ali steps through the door. I hesitate for a moment but then follow him. I'm expecting him and the house to disappear at any moment, but they don't.

Ali and I are standing on a beautiful faded carpet in front of the desk behind which the old man has sat down again. The room is full of books from floor to ceiling. There's a shelf on the wall, on which there are rolled parchments, and there's a cabinet full of objects: coins, tiny oil lamps, a leather sandal, bronze arrow heads, a bead necklace, an axe head, a clay figure of a bull. A small fire is spitting and cracking in the grate. The room smells of tobacco.

The old man is looking at us in amazement. His face is deathly pale.

"Greetings, beloved Baba," says Ali.

I don't know what language they are speaking but I can understand every word.

The old man's voice wobbles as he says, "Can you come a little closer? You are outside the circle of light. I cannot see you properly."

We step forward until our legs are touching his desk. Ali leans across the desk and kisses his father's hand and touches that hand to his forehead.

The old man's eyes are shining. He is shaking. Tears are running down his face. "So, the English woman was right. My son, it is wonderful to see you. I never thought to see you again."

I can feel Ali trembling next to me. The tears are streaking down his face as well. He looks terrified. He turns to me and says, "I do not understand. What is happening? Why is it like this?"

And once again, I don't know how to tell him, how to make him understand. I put my hand on his shoulder to comfort him.

For what seems like a long time but may be only a few seconds, the old man gazes into the face of his son. Ali doesn't speak again.

And then the old man turns to look at me. He smiles, "And who is your friend, my son?"

Something about the way he asks this really scares me.

His words have broken a spell.

It's as though I'd forgotten that I'm standing with a ghost in a house that isn't there being introduced to an old man who isn't there either.

And suddenly, I'm more frightened than I've ever been in my whole life. My legs are shaking and I feel I could collapse on the carpet at any moment.

I say something like, "I'm sorry. I must go." And, without waiting for a reply, I turn and run out of the room.

As I leave, there's a shadowy figure coming up the path. It stops as if to greet me, but I brush past it. It feels like I've touched an electric cobweb. I run back through the orchard, jumping the stream as if it isn't there.

I don't want to attempt to walk through the barrier, so I climb over it, scratching my hands and face.

I really need to be with Mum and Dad. I run down the road, owls are hooting in the trees. I turn in at the gate to the villa and jump down the steps, nearly falling as I do so.

But I don't get a chance to tell Mum and Dad what's happened because they're sitting at the outside table with Mr Basak and a woman with flaming red hair. Three blonde children are asleep on the floor.

Listening

My English is not good, but it is better than I let the guests (or the Basaks) know. This can be useful. Sometimes they say things in front of me that they would not say if they knew I understood. This might enable me to do the little things that earn a better tip at the end of the week. Maybe by making a present of a few cucumbers from my garden, or putting more petals on the bedspreads. Maybe I hear them say something like the way I fold their towels is a 'nice touch'. This is valuable information.

Also, my look of incomprehension prevents them from asking me too many questions, from prying into my life. I am not, after all, part of what I believe is called the 'Turkey experience'. Mr Basak does not pay me anything like enough for that.

Sometimes, of course, I hear things that the guests very definitely would not want me to hear. I hear the bitterness of wives who have do all the shopping and cooking even though they are on holiday. Husbands complaining about the selfishness and lack of discipline of their children. Children saying insolent, disrespectful things to their parents and to each other.

I just keep my head down and act as if I have no idea what is being said. For all they know, "hello' and 'thank you' are my only English words.

Maggie and Steve are not like this, but even they sometimes talk to each other as though I'm not there. In the past couple of days they've been talking a lot about this person called Anneke, who is staying with her children in the villa on the corner that is owned by the Dutch people who never come here. It seems that Maggie likes her very much. Steve has not yet met her but teases Maggie about her, saying things like he can't wait to meet her.

I have to admit that a little part of me envies Maggie's relationship with Steve. They appear to like each other so much. It is not so in our house, where I am forced to make all the important decisions while pretending that Urfuz is the one who has made them. When I married him I did not realize what a passive man he is. Unable to make things happen. He makes me want to scream. And he has been very strange recently. As if there is something on his mind. I don't ask him what the matter is because the truth is I don't want to know.

The more I see of Maggie the more convinced I am that, although she seems cheerful and busy, there is some sadness in her life. I also think that, taking all things together, she is probably a good person. I would not say the same about this Anneke. I know that Urfuz would say that I am becoming an old prude (let him think what he likes) but I cannot approve of her. She is the type of woman I do not like. From what I had been able to gather, there have been a number of men in her life, and her attitude towards her children seemed very casual. I thought she must be selfish and self-obsessed. I was sure that I would not warm to her if I met her, and I was right.

I was just leaving after cleaning the villa this morning when Maggie asked me—using a sequence of mimes, a bit of pointing at her watch, a lot of smiling and some truly terrible Turkish from her phrasebook—if I could spare a couple of hours this afternoon to help out because Anneke and her children were coming to supper. The money is always useful and so—though a series of mimes, and a lot of smiles and no English at all—I agreed.

When I got back to the villa around four, Steve had just returned from the supermarket with enough shopping for a week. Maggie and I helped him carry it down the stairs and into the kitchen. He asked what else he could do. He said nothing would be too much trouble and Maggie gave him a warning look. I think she must have asked him to arrange the cutlery and crockery on the table. I say 'I think' because although Steve took the stuff out there, he left it on the table in a heap and disappeared. We only found out when he got back half an hour later that he'd suddenly decided to go for a walk and had dropped in on Mr Basak. Maggie mimed a person walking for my benefit—although it was more like a person marching.

Maggie is not good at giving instructions and so it was hard to find out what she wanted me to do. I thought that maybe I could clean the bathroom and the toilet (even though I had already cleaned them in the morning) but it seemed that this was not right. She said, "Don't worry about that. I'd rather have you helping me in the kitchen." Of course, I couldn't let her know that I understood. So, what followed was a mime of someone peeling vegetables. If I hadn't already known what she wanted, I might have thought she was miming someone with a rash on their hands. Or putting on a pair of tight gloves. And just to make sure I understood, she took the bucket and mop out of my hands and put them in the cupboard under the stairs. I'm sure she was trying to be kind, but she was leaving me with nothing to do.

So, for the next couple of hours, we worked in the kitchen, peeling and preparing. Maggie put some music on and Steve offered—by miming and pointing—to make me tea or coffee. I felt shy and ill at ease but it was easy money.

The aubergines were sliced, salads were made and in the fridge, the chicken was ready for the oven and I was preparing to leave, when this Anneke person turned up with her children. She is as beautiful as Maggie says and so are her children. When Maggie introduced us, instead of shaking hands she kissed me. I was surprised. She is not my friend. I did not smile. As I could not let my disapproval show, I tried to look distracted.

I think Maggie may have noticed my discomfort and she asked Anneke if she and the children could pick a few flowers from the garden to decorate the table. I wanted to say that I did not think Mr Basak would want his plants picked but I couldn't of course. I hung the tea towels on the line and said goodbye to Maggie and Steve and was just walking out of the door when Anneke and her children came in carrying armloads of flowers. They must have picked half the flowers in the garden. Maggie said something like, "Oh dear, that's more than I needed." I thought it best if I said nothing and so I left.

I think Mr Basak is going to be upset. And I know Urfuz is. He is always talking about the garden as if it is his. I only hope he doesn't want to talk to me about it. I hope he realizes by now that I'm not someone who cares much what he thinks or feels.

Skinny dipping

This has been one of the strangest evenings of my life. Or, to be accurate, given that it's nearly six in the morning, yesterday evening was one of the strangest evenings of my life. I wish Seyhan had been here to share it with me, but I suppose if she had been, it might not have happened as it did. Indeed, it might not have happened at all. I certainly would not have done what I did.

I have long accepted that when you rent properties you have to be prepared to become involved to a degree in the lives of your guests. But I never expected anything as complicated or as emotional or as strange as what happened. I need to work out how much of this to tell Seyhan and how much to keep secret. There are things that she must never know. I can't decide if she did know whether she would be angry or whether she would laugh. Either response would be difficult to endure.

I was in the garden late this afternoon when there was a knock at the door in the wall. It was Steve returning the Agatha Christie novel that I had lent him. I could tell at once that he does not admire it as I do. I asked him what he thought of it and he said, "You have to remember that I read it with a slight hangover so it's all a bit of a blur. But I seem to recall that there was quite a lot of psychology in there and a fair bit about moustaches. Oh, and apparently glandular secretions are to blame for lots of serial killings."

I did not think this merited a response.

Then he said, "I've come to ask you a favour."

"Anything, my friend." For some reason I imagined he was going to ask to borrow something; perhaps a bottle of tonic water.

"I was wondering if you would come to supper with us this evening. Maggie has made friends with Anneke, the woman staying at the villa on the corner, and I thought it would be nice if you joined us. It would be great to have another man there for when they start dancing around their handbags. And I could reciprocate your hospitality of the other night, although maybe we should be a little more circumspect. Do you know that word?"

"It is a word I have encountered in Ms Christie's work," I said, rather prissily it's true, but I am proud of my English, although I did not fully understand the reference to dancing and handbags.

I was instinctively reluctant to say yes. Something was telling me that it would be wise to keep my distance. It was one thing having Steve here for a drink on his own, it would be quite another to get involved in the life of his family and friends.

"You are very kind," I said, "but I have much paperwork to do so maybe I should say no."

"Oh, come on, Kemal. Please. I'm sure the paperwork can wait. Just come for a while and if it's too boring you can leave as soon as we've eaten. Besides, it will be a chance for you to sample Turkish cooking. I bought all sorts of exciting things at the supermarket today. *Please.* You know you want to."

This made me smile and so, in the end, I said that I would. "After all, I don't want to miss out on the chance to sample Turkish cooking."

"Great. Thanks."

Steve left immediately, presumably so that I wouldn't have a chance to change my mind.

"See you at eight."

I have to admit than in spite of my reservations, part of me was pleased to have been asked. It's not as if we get that many invitations. I suppose people think I am a man who likes to keep himself to himself. I notice when I drink *çay* in the café in the village, the other men seem to be uncomfortable in my presence. They clearly feel that I am not one of them. Even after living here for all these years, I'm still seen as an incomer.

Of course, the moment Steve left I realized that there were many things I should have asked him. Should I bring something? What should I wear? And so on. I know that British people are capable of great formality on occasions, the problem is that they are also capable of great informality on others. How is a non-Brit to decide which is which?

I could imagine Seyhan saying, "Only a great fool like you would worry about such things. Take some flowers and go as you are. Of course there will not be any formality. But maybe, on second thoughts, change your T shirt, it is too reminiscent of the fact that you have been digging the garden in it."

In the end I decided to take the first part of her advice and ignore the second. I gathered a bunch of lilies and oleanders from the garden and wrapped them with ribbon. Then I showered and shaved and rubbed my chin with lemon oil. I put on my white silk shirt with a dark blue silk tie.

I could hear Seyhan in my ear, "You look like you are going to meet your bank manager." But I ignored her. There was nothing I could do about my hair; there never is.

At one minute to eight I closed the door behind me. If I had known then what I know now, I might have returned twenty seconds later. But perhaps not, after all.

The light was fading as I went through the door in the wall. When I reached the pool I could see that there were a number of children in it. This Anneke person's, I assumed. They turned to stare at me and I had to suppress the urge to say, "You do realize that this is my pool? I built it." But I smiled and said hello and they smiled and waved back and then forgot all about me. I was concerned that there were no adults supervising them, which is strictly against the rules printed on the sign by the pool.

When I reached the house there was no one in sight. But it was obvious that Maggie had gone to a lot of trouble. The outside table was laid for supper with plates and glasses, it seemed that every candle in the house was on the table and lit. (What will they do if—*when*—there is a power cut? I sometimes think I am the only person in the world who thinks ahead, who anticipates difficulties.)

The table was decorated with heaps of oleanders and white lilies, all of which must have been picked been picked from the garden. There were cotton napkins, which she must have bought from the market, by every place. They certainly don't belong to the house.

Something grey and sleek darted between my legs and made me jump. It was that damned cat.

I could hear voices inside and the sounds of cooking. I knocked on the door.

The second it opened, I realized that Seyhan was right and I was wrong. I was overdressed. Significantly. The door had been opened by a young woman with more red hair than she knew what to do with. She was wearing one of the smallest bikinis I have ever seen and a see-through sarong that was knotted around her waist. Round her neck were half a dozen huge necklaces. Her eyes were laughing as if at some private joke.

"Hello, you must be Kemal," come in. And with that, she put her hands on my shoulders and kissed me on both cheeks.

I was so surprised that I didn't know where to look. I was conscious of staring at her so turned my gaze to a place just above her head. However, in that short time I had registered a slim freckled body. I couldn't help it. She had obviously had too much sun; her nose was red and there was a patch of pink skin at her throat.

Maggie confirmed my suspicions about having got the dress code wrong. She was wearing a T shirt with a picture of David Bowie on the front and what appeared to be a pair of Steve's sneakers. Certainly they were way too big for her. She had apparently forgotten to get dressed below the waist.

"Hi, Kemal. You look marvelous. Have a drink."

She also kissed me on both cheeks and handed me what turned out to be a glass of champagne. I gave her the flowers, which she said were lovely.

"Steve will be down in a moment. Typical man, he's left it late to have his shower. And while we are on the subject of Steve, he told me that you led him astray the other night.

Forced him to drink alcohol against his will. What do you have to say for yourself?"

I knew that she was joking of course, but I was so flustered by the situation, that I found myself apologizing as though I thought she had been serious.

She and Anneke both laughed.

I felt gauche and embarrassed. I couldn't think of anything to say but it didn't seem to matter because Maggie and Anneke rattled on to one another as they carried on with the cooking.

I heard a door shut upstairs and then Steve appeared wearing a pair of shorts, a polo shirt and a native American headdress of brightly coloured feathers. This was not what I had expected.

"How?" he said. I didn't understand what he meant.

"This belongs to one of Anneke's kids," he explained. "I've just borrowed it. Looks rather chic don't you think?"

I said that I thought it looked very nice and everybody laughed.

Steve said, "I see I've got some catching up to do. Would you be wanting a top up at all?"

I said that I would and everybody laughed some more.

Anneke said to Steve, "Could you and Kemal perhaps ask the children to come out of the pool and get ready for supper? I need to help Maggie with getting everything on the table."

So Steve and I hauled the kids out of the pool and wrapped them in towels. They didn't particularly want to come out but the promise of food seemed to swing it. I thought one little girl, Elsje I think, said to Steve in almost flawless English that they hadn't had a proper meal since they left Amsterdam, but I must have misheard.

We all sat at the table, the kids dripping. Steve, who was still wearing the headdress, filled everyone's glasses and we started to eat. I imagined that the kids would be fidgety and annoying but in fact they were absolutely focused on eating. There was no time to squabble or get on anyone's nerves. It was a serious race to see which of them could get outside the most calories in the shortest time. Plateful after plateful of food disappeared under their silent and sustained onslaught.

The food was excellent: aubergine bake, a stew of peppers and tomatoes, sautéed potatoes, grilled chicken, a rice salad, flatbreads, dishes of almonds and olives. I was starting to relax and enjoy myself.

I noticed that Maggie was mainly watching the children eating and that Steve was mainly watching Maggie.

I also noticed that Anneke wasn't eating very much, although she was drinking rather a lot of wine. I couldn't follow everything she said—her accent seemed to get stronger as the evening went on. She spoke a lot about someone she called a 'total bastard' and she told a very long story about how she had been asked out to dinner by the lead singer of a famous Dutch rock band, called *Nutteloos Muzikanten*. I asked her what that meant and I thought she said, "It means 'useless musicians'." So maybe I misunderstood. Apparently he had been very importunate in his requests to take her out but she had resisted his overtures out of misplaced loyalty to the total bastard. And now she wishes she had the opportunity again. At least, I think that's what she said.

Steve did not appear to be paying any attention to any of this, and seemed happy for me to be the target of Anneke's reminiscences. It was clear that he would not be coming to my rescue any time soon. I have to confess that when she started to list total bastard's major faults at some length, I started to think of something else. Of Seyhan in Ankara.

Out of the corner of my eye, I saw the grey cat take up a position a short distance from the table, waiting for any scraps. It was as though it knew that at that moment I was powerless to act against it.

I thought, "You think you are very clever, don't you. But you wait, my opportunity will come."

The cat ignored me and appeared to be staring hard at one end of the table where Anneke's children were stuffing their faces. I could not see what was so fascinating but the cat was riveted.

The eating and drinking continued for some time. The children in particular ate an extraordinary amount. After Maggie and Anneke had cleared away the main course, they produced a box of baklava, a fruit salad and a plate of mint-flavoured Turkish delight. The children fell on this as if they had not already eaten their own weight. Maggie looked happy as she watched them stuffing their faces. Anneke was in the middle of another anecdote about the impact she had made on some man or other but no one seemed very interested and she didn't seem to care whether or not they were.

Steve didn't miss an opportunity to fill everyone's glasses about every ten minutes and no one seemed inclined to try to stop him.

Eventually, however, the eating had to stop. The children were exhausted and Anneke said that she must take them home.

But she said it in a way that made it clear that she was happy to have her mind changed.

Maggie said, "Oh, there's no need to go yet. The children can have a sleep here and Steve will help you get them back later. Won't you Steve?"

Steve said that he would be 'honoured'.

Maggie and Anneke made up a bed for the children out of all the floor cushions in the sitting room. But the children said they didn't want to sleep there. They begged to be allowed to sleep in the porch so that they could see us. So, Maggie dragged the cushion outside and improvised a mosquito net with what appeared to be one of the curtains from the second bedroom. The children stumbled from the table, fell onto the cushions in a heap, still in their wet swimming costumes, and were instantly asleep. It was like flicking a switch.

That damned cat crept closer and took up guard duty right next to the pile of sleeping children. This time, it did look at me, as if to say, "You can't lay a finger on me with these people here. They would never forgive you."

Checking that no one was looking, I mouthed the words, "You wait," at it.

Maybe it was my imagination, but the cat appeared to have been thriving on the food Maggie has been giving it. It looked fatter than before and unbearably smug. My fingers were itching but, at the same time, part of me—in spite of myself—admired its courage and its insolence. I realized what I had perhaps not seen before: this is no ordinary cat. This is a very special cat. I still intend to kill it, however, before it gets at my chickens. Special won't save it.

Maggie and Anneke went inside to make coffee. We could hear them laughing together. Steve refilled my glass. I intended to say no but somehow I let him go ahead.

The women must have turned on the iPod because the sound of country and western music suddenly filled the air. I was worried that it would wake the children, but they simply stirred and snuffled.

After coffee, Anneke produced a rolled-up cigarette. She offered one to me but I said that I would be happier with a cigar if Maggie would permit it. Maggie said that she would be 'thrilled', that cigars reminded her of her father. While I was lighting it, Anneke took a couple of puffs of her cigarette and then handed it to Maggie who also took a couple of puffs before handing it to Steve. He looked at it for a moment and then at Maggie, then he shrugged his shoulders, put it in his mouth, drew deeply and started coughing.

It wasn't until this moment that I realized they were smoking drugs. I was shocked; after all, this is my property and they are middle-aged people not teenagers. However, although I was their guest, in a sense they were my guests, so I didn't know how to respond. I thought this young woman had taken an absurd risk bringing drugs into the country. But I would have looked ridiculous if I'd said something like, 'I forbid this' and gone home. (I think my fear of appearing ridiculous is fuelled by my conviction that I so often do.) It was while I was trying to think of an appropriate response that Steve handed the cigarette to me.

The only explanation I have for what happened next is that I was flustered, did not know how to react to the situation, had

had my glass refilled many times by Steve and did not wish to give offence to my host/guests. Before I realized what I was doing I put it in my mouth and dragged on it. I am sure this would not have happened had Seyhan been there to guide me. The smoke was harsh but fortunately I was totally unaffected by it. I felt ashamed but I also felt pleased with myself. I handed it back to Anneke, praying that it would not come my way again. Unfortunately, it did, but I was by now confident that I was immune. I puffed on it once more and handed it to Maggie who finished it.

We sat for a while with our thoughts. No one seemed to want to say anything much. Bats were swooping silently over our heads. Above them, the stars were winking brightly.

And then Anneke got up and started dancing to the music, stretching out her arms and swaying her hips. She is very boring but she is also very beautiful and I found it hard to keep my eyes off her. Maggie soon joined her. Every time she lifted her arms above her head, her T shirt rode dangerously high up her legs. I was alarmed for her. She was threatened with exposure.

And then—I cannot explain how or why this happened, it is certainly not something I would usually do—I loosened my tie and joined the ladies. I wished to demonstrate Turkish dancing to them. I held Maggie's right hand in my left and Anneke's left hand in my right. We stood in a line and I tried to teach them some elementary steps. It did not go particularly well. We kept getting out of sync and both Maggie and Anneke kept laughing, so not much dancing was done. Finally, Steve downed whatever was in his glass and started doing a war dance, going round and round us.

I looked at the children but they did not stir although there was real anger in the cat's eyes. It was clearly concerned for its charges. But that won't save it either.

And then, as if this was not strange enough, something truly unexpected and extraordinary occurred. Anneke stopped dancing, unwound her sarong, stripped off her bikini, stood momentarily naked in the moonlight and then ran off down the path towards the pool. Seconds later we heard a splash. There was silence for a moment—I noticed that the music had stopped—and then Maggie said, "Shall we join her?" Steve looked at me as if to say, "Are you OK with this?" But once again, I did not know how to respond.

In fact, matters were immediately taken out of my hands because Maggie then tugged her T shirt over her head—I couldn't help but notice that she was more substantial than Anneke but equally beautiful—and, still wearing Steve's absurd sneakers, ran off down the path. There was a second splash. Followed by laughter.

Steve said, "What do you think?" but before I could answer he appeared to make up his mind. He solemnly removed his headdress and put it on the table. "Help yourself to another drink, I'll be back in a minute." Then he peeled off his clothes and ran down the path whooping. Third splash.

So, I was left alone with the cat and the sleeping children. I felt ridiculous but I also felt envious of the fact that the other three were so obviously having fun. Had Seyhan been here, that would have been that. But I wanted to prove to them that I was not the old stick-in-the-mud—the old *tutucu*—that they so obviously thought me. I also felt resentful that Steve had not tried to include me. I set off towards the pool still fully clothed. When I got there, the other three were splashing and laughing in the night air. The scent of the oleanders and lilies was strong and the stars were perfect. The pool lights had turned the water a milky blue. I made up my mind. I quickly pulled off my clothes and jumped in—which is strictly against the rules—with the fourth and mightiest splash and to the applause of the others. But even as I was in mid air, I thought, "What would Seyhan say if she could see me at this moment?"

A quarter of an hour later we were again sitting around the table, wrapped in towels. The children had not stirred. Steve filled everyone's glass. I felt extraordinarily relaxed.

And then, Anneke asked Maggie, "Where is your son Matt? Why is he not here with us?"

I was astonished when she said this. Maybe I had misunderstood. I felt certain that I had misunderstood so many of the things she had said.

There was a silence for a moment. I saw Steve look at Maggie.

In a very quiet voice she said, "I think he might be in his room. Or maybe he's gone for a walk."

Again, I thought I must have misheard or misunderstood.

I could feel a tension between her and Steve, but apparently Anneke couldn't. "But if he is in his room, why has he not joined us?"

Again Steve looked at Maggie.

She said in the same little voice, "He is not very sociable. He is shy. He likes it in his room."

"Maybe I could persuade him to come out," said Anneke,

standing up.

There was a silence. Then Steve put his arm round Maggie and said, "Come on, luvvie, this can't go on."

All at once, Maggie began to cry; huge gulping sobs. There was nothing well mannered or decorous about her crying she just fell apart in front of us. Dissolved.

The damned cat stirred, sat up and looked at her.

I didn't know what to think or what to do.

Anneke started to apologise: "Maggie, I'm sorry... What is wrong?... Have I said something wrong?... I'm so sorry."

Maggie, turned to Steve: "You tell them."

Steve said, "Are you sure?"

"You may as well."

"The thing is," said Steve, "we don't have a son called Matt. We don't have a son at all."

Of course, I knew this.

"That's not true," said Maggie, "we did have a son, but we lost him."

"OK, we did," said Steve. "On our first trip to Turkey, years ago, Maggie was pregnant. Everyone said it was fine to travel. That she would be OK on the plane. But on our second day of the holiday, she had a miscarriage. It was a boy. He was perfect. We were devastated but we had to get on with things."

Maggie interrupted him, "Steve is being kind as he is always and has always been kind. It was sixteen years ago. He was devastated and got on with things. I was devastated and completely failed to get on with things. I really thought I wouldn't be able to hold my life together. Everyone was incredibly kind and I was hardly the first woman ever to have a miscarriage. But knowing this didn't help at all. The only thing that helped was talking about our baby as if he was alive, as if things hadn't gone wrong. Obviously, I couldn't do this in public where everyone knew what had happened. But at home, I could pretend. Steve instinctively felt that this was a terrible idea, but because he is kind, he indulged me. And it enabled me to continue functioning."

Anneke was crying and had her arms around Maggie. I felt like crying too.

The wretched cat (it should be counting the days and hours left to it) suddenly got up, walked a couple of metres, arched its back and hissed at nothing. The fur was standing up in spikes on its back. Then it went back to the children and curled up again.

Steve said, "Maggie was so raw, I had to go along with it. If that was how she was going to cope, then I felt I had to help her. After a time, real life started to intervene again and Maggie seemed to have less need of the pretence. But every year, we come back to Turkey for a couple of weeks, where no one knows us and Maggie can set her imagination free. She can pretend that our son is with us. After all, who's going to know?"

Maggie said, "When we come here, I feel he is so close to me. Over the years, he's gone from being an imaginary baby to an imaginary toddler, to an imaginary child, to an imaginary teenager. I've imagined a whole life for him: friends, school, I've been able to picture him so clearly at every stage of his life. I know everything about him: what he smells like, how his hair feels, how he always scuffs the heels of his shoes, that one crooked tooth. Everything. He has been always with me. It's hard to see how a mother could ever be closer to her son.

Besides, who are we hurting? You are the first people I've ever told this to."

Anneke said, "I think the person this is hurting is you."

I thought this was very brave of her. It was exactly what I had been thinking, but I would not have dared to say it.

Maggie looked at her for a moment and then she said, "You are right. Of course, I know that. But I have always felt that it was good for me as well. It has always felt so real. Particularly when we come to this country. I'm not sure that he could have been any more real to me even if he had lived."

Not being real

When Mum said that about me having died before I was even a baby, I couldn't understand what was going on. I thought it must be some horrible joke that had gone wrong. But no one was laughing.

I said, "Mum, that's not funny."

But no one took any notice. No one was looking at me. It was as though I wasn't there.

I said it again, louder but still no one took any notice. They were all trying to comfort Mum. The woman with the mad red hair had her arms round her and was crying as well. Mr Basak looked as though he would much rather be somewhere else. Anywhere else. He and Dad looked at each other helplessly.

I started to scream: "I'm here. It's me. I'm here. Please don't pretend I'm not. I'm here. I am here. You can't ignore me."

I thought that if I went on shouting, they would have to stop this awful pretence and recognize that I really was there. If they didn't, I would wake the children up. But all that happened was that the cat climbed off the pile of sleeping children, looked straight into my eyes, arched its back and hissed at me. It was behaving as if it thought I was some sort of threat to the children it was guarding. The children didn't stir.

I screamed for what seemed like hours but nobody took any

notice. In the end, I was so exhausted I had to give up.

I had to accept that they couldn't see and hear me. This was the most terrifying thing that had ever happened to me. But what Mum was saying couldn't be true. Of course I exist. Of course I'm me.

My heart was beating so fast I thought I might have a heart attack. I could feel my blood pounding in my ears. My head was splitting with a migraine. Stars and spirals were flashing in front of my eyes. I felt like I was dying.

And then I thought: "Of course I exist. I live in the world. And the things I do make a difference to the world. For example, I've carved my name on the tomb wall. Ali and I have dug in the garden."

In some strange way, this thought comforted me. If I could prove it, everyone else would have to accept it.

The sky was beginning to lighten on the other side of the valley when I left all those people consoling Mum (who was going to console me?) and climbed the stairs to the upper track. Even though it was after four, the air was warm. A few stars were still visible.

By the time I reached the edge of the cliff, the sky in the east behind me was a blaze of scarlet. Fingers of pale light stretched across the sky in front of me. The stars had gone.

Again, I felt the urge to jump. Much stronger this time. After all, what did I have to lose?

As I looked down I thought I caught a glimpse of a man with red hair standing absolutely still by the river and staring at me. He was stocky and ugly and seemed to be wearing some kind of tunic. He could have been a figure of fun but there was nothing funny about him. In fact, he was terrifying. Radiating power and threat. I couldn't see him properly in the dim light but for a moment I thought he raised his arm as if he was going to wave or something. But when I looked again there was no sign of him. Perhaps I had imagined him.

I climbed down to the tomb ledge but did not make any attempt to do it safely. What was the worst that could happen? But, of course, I found myself safely on the stone ledge by the fig tree.

Now that I am here, I'm scared to enter the tomb. In the end, I dive in, not bothering to hold onto the fig tree for balance. Because the sun isn't yet fully up, the inside is pitch black. I can't see anything. I'm going to have to wait a bit longer.

I sit on the ledge like I saw Ali do, with my legs dangling in space. I am very afraid, but heights are just about the last thing I'm afraid of. I look for the scary man with the red hair. I think that maybe I can see two tiny figures in the distance, heading towards the sea. They are too far away for me to call to them, and what would I say to them even if I could?

It's already hot. The tomb is directly behind me and will be well lit by now. All I have to do is turn round. But that is just so hard. The hardest thing I have ever had to do. But then I turn and I climb back inside.

Everything is as it was the first time I saw it. The broken terracotta on the floor. The dust. The scorch marks on the ceiling. But when I look where I scratched my name there is nothing. The wall is blank. I am filled with despair.

I lie on the floor in the dust, my knees tucked up to my

chest. For a while, there is nothing in my head. It's empty. Like a stripped white room. But then images and memories start to flood back. Not in any particular order; just bits and pieces. Fragments.

A grey cat with grey eyes. Stalls loaded with tomatoes. Mum trying to find out about Elif's life. Lights twinkling on water. A soldier far from home. Red, yellow and green kites against a blue sky. Someone jumping off a bridge. A silver coin with the image of a man wearing a lion skin headdress. Rain streaming down the road. Storks climbing staircases of air. Olive trees shifting in the wind like waves on the sea. An old man with a hooked nose and a heartbroken face. A box full of chicks. Dad with the sea not reaching his knees. Ali drinking from his leather water bag. An owl screeching in the darkness. Mum lying on her sunbed. Dad reading Agatha Christie in his hammock. Oranges in the dust. Ali falling. Someone singing in German. Ruined houses. A small brown man with a large moustache hiding in the garden. Terracotta specks in the soil. An old man on a tractor. Swallows clinging to moving reeds. An ancient pavement leading downhill. The look in a turtle's eyes. A guide book to Ephesus. Stars in the shape of a bird. A broken wooden door hanging off its hinges. Trees like flames. Blood trickling down my leg. An eagle's nest. A chain link fence. Pirates with plastic cutlasses. Goats crossing a road. Clouds building up until they threaten to cover the sky and then collapsing. The look on Hello's face when Dad hugged him. Lightning flickering in the mountains. Two young men dangling fearlessly from ropes. A brushwood barrier. Three hawks quartering a field. The mad face of a hermit. Hens scratching in the dirt. A waterfall. A fig tree.

I can remember all these things and so many more. But all these memories are from the last few days. When I try to think about what came before that, my mind is blank.

There is nothing before last week.

And the more I remember of the things that have happened since we came here, the more it starts to make a terrifying sense. When we went to the beach and I wanted lemonade, it never arrived. I did not drink it. The conversations that Mum and Dad had as though they were alone. Why they didn't question me about the stone on the windowsill. Why they lay by the pool as if there were just the two of them.

All I can bring back from the time before this week is a dirty grey light with shapes, which might be people, or which might be something else, moving around in the background.

It's like watching a play happening behind a thick curtain. I think I can hear the faintest murmuring of voices. I think I can hear Mum calling my name. But I can't be sure. I think I can hear the beating of a heart. Perhaps it's mine. Or perhaps it's two hearts.

Other than that, there's nothing.

I stand on the ledge of the tomb and look outwards at the waking world. Everything is so beautiful; the light, the shapes, the movement, the warmth. But I am no part of any of this.

I let myself drop headfirst. The ground rushes up towards me. I'm knocked sideways by a sudden gust of wind. I'm looking forward to the moment when my skull splits on the waiting rocks. And then… nothing.

I'm back inside the tomb again, looking out at a world in

which everything is going on as usual. I can see trees moving. I watch clouds track across the sky. I can hear birdsong. A butterfly passes the entrance of the tomb. It's just a normal day behaving as normal days behave. And I am no part of it.

I jump again and the same thing happens. The ground rushes up to smash me and then I'm back in here watching the world.

And again.

There's only one other place I can go and that's back to the garden. The only person who knows that I exist is a ghost but going back there seems to be my last chance to confirm myself.

I climb out of the rock tomb and scale the cliff. As I walk back through the trees, I have an intense, painful sense of how beautiful the forest is. How the trees move in the breeze like dancers, how the sun breaks through the canopy and spotlights the ferns.

I clamber over the stone threshold into the garden. I call for Ali but there is no reply.

It's very hot in here and the light is dazzling. The crickets have fallen silent and the butterflies are too hot to fly—they cling to the flowers flexing their wings. The only things that are moving are the three hawks which flash silently from one corner of the garden to another. As I watch, one of them catches a large blue dragonfly in its talons. Without ever slowing down, it eats it while still on the wing. Flicking from here to there. Nothing to it. The only sound is the crackling of the dried thistles as their seed pods expand in the heat.

At least I know that Ali and I acted on this garden. We've dug half a dozen holes and pulled large pieces of stone out of the ground. But when I look for these holes, I can't find them. The garden is deserted, the ground undisturbed. There's not the faintest scratch mark on the surface to suggest that we were ever here. There is a large piece of stone leaning against a tree, but there is no scar in the bark. It's just a ruined garden. A ruined garden in which nothing has happened.

I'm exhausted and empty and filled with despair. I think about going back to the villa to have one more go at making myself known, making myself felt. But I don't know what I'll find there. And I'm too tired.

So I lie in the shade of the beautiful trees and I look up at the sky. It's so intensely blue that it breaks my heart.

It's all over.

I love you

God, last night was awful. It was horrible to see Maggie crying so hard. Still heartbroken after all these years.

But I guess it was bound to happen sometime—and there is a large part of me that recognizes that it may have been a good thing. That part of Maggie wanted it to happen. Why else would she have invited Anneke to the villa? If she hadn't, she would have got away with it.

But the reality is that we couldn't go on pretending about Matt. Even just between the two of us. It was preventing us ever moving on. Has been preventing us for all these years. If only we'd been able to have another kid. But it didn't happen. Maybe because neither of us could let Matt go. Neither of us really *wanted* to let him go.

After I got Maggie to bed, Kemal and I took Anneke and the kids back to her villa, although she was all for sleeping on the floor with them and the mangy cat. The kids hardly stirred when we picked them up. I had the little boy asleep on my shoulder and Kemal tucked a little girl under each arm.

Anneke is a bit of a pain and some of her stories need tightening up but I think her heart's in the right place. She was almost as upset as Maggie—I don't think it was just the dope—and seemed really to feel for her even though they've only known each other a couple of days. She didn't talk much on the way back. I definitely prefer her when she isn't in the middle of one of her stories about how irresistible she is to all sorts of semi-famous blokes I've never heard of. Maybe she really believes it, but maybe she just needs a narrative to compensate for the fact that total bastard has taken himself off.

The villa was in utter chaos. Every surface seemed to be covered in kids' clothes and wet towels, books and toys. There were dirty plates and cups on the table, and food all over the floor. So maybe Anneke isn't managing to bring up three kids on her own quite as smoothly as Maggie imagines.

The kids' bedroom wasn't any better. Looked like a bomb had gone off. It was hard to see how they could have got so much stuff onto the plane. There seemed to be more clothes, toys and assorted bric-a-brac in the room than they can possibly have put in their suitcases. Where had it all come from? It was a kind of minor miracle; creating something out of nothing. Anneke and her sprogs may actually be challenging the laws of thermodynamics.

Maybe because they'd eaten so much at supper, the kids didn't wake up when we tipped them into bed—two in one, one in the other. We covered them up with blankets and Anneke kissed each of their heads.

Kemal and I were just about to make a tactical withdrawal when Anneke asked us to stay for 'just one drink'. She seemed so desperate and so reluctant to be left on her own that we could only say yes.

She produced a bottle of Bols and three grubby glasses, which we took outside and sat by her pool. It was getting light and was deliciously warm. The pool was full of junk, including a semi–deflated crocodile that watched us suspiciously out of a luminous eye. The expression on its face was oddly sad, as if it was burdened with some knowledge not available to the rest of us. It was as if it was saying, "You don't know what it's like to feel all the air leaking out of you."

None of us seemed to want to talk much but the silence felt oddly companionable given that only a few days ago none of us had ever set eyes on each other. There was nothing to drink with the Bols, so we took it straight. I didn't have the energy to look for a lemon tree at that time in the morning.

Anneke started to roll another spliff, but neither Kemal nor I thought it was a very good idea to share it. So she smoked the whole thing on her own.

I'm ashamed to say that one glass of Bols was followed by another and then a third. I knew at the time that this wasn't a particularly good idea, but even as my brain was telling me this, my hand was pouring it into my glass.

I'm not sure whether it was Kemal or me who first noticed that Anneke had fallen asleep in her chair, glass in hand, her hair covering her face.

I tried to wake her. I put my hand on her shoulder and shook her gently. Nothing. I shook her a tiny bit harder. She opened her eyes—they really are the most amazing blue—looked at me and said, "I love you." Then she closed her eyes again.

Kemal took over. He put his hand on her shoulder and shook her gently. Nothing. He shook her a tiny bit harder. She opened her eyes—which were still the most amazing blue—looked at him and said, "I love you." Then she closed her eyes again.

So, I took hold of her under her arms and Kemal picked up

her feet and we carried her, still unconscious, into the house. Not that we were all that steady on our feet. It was probably a matter of luck that the three of us didn't end up in the pool again.

Her bedroom was even more of a mess than the kids'. Clothes, make up, wet towels, full ash trays and empty wine bottles were strewn everywhere. The bed was unmade. We laid her down as gently as we could and covered her with a sheet. She opened her eyes for a moment, looked at us and said, "I love you both," and closed her eyes again.

As I plugged in the mosquito repellant, she started to snore. Surprisingly loudly: zzzz... ZZzz... ZZZZ... NNGRKK.

She is very gorgeous when she is asleep but better with the sound turned down.

I didn't mention it to Kemal but part of me wanted to stay there for a while to make sure that she and the kids were OK. If I hadn't been so pissed, I might even have done a spot of clearing up. Maggie's right. Anneke's so vulnerable that she makes you want to protect her. I think maybe Kemal felt the same thing. But there was nothing we could do, so we left.

As we walked back to the villa I could feel that he wanted to ask me more about what had happened. Maybe commiserate with me. Try to understand what had been going on. But I wasn't in the mood for it.

It was now well after five and the most amazing sunrise was happening across the valley. Real look-at-me stuff.

Suddenly, Kemal started talking about what he calls his 'ghost children'. Apparently, he never wanted kids because he would have had to share old Seyhan with them. He says that instead he has been living with these ghost children—the children they never had—for so many years. He says that sometimes they seem to fill the house, that there's hardly room for him to move or breathe. That somehow, in spite of all his planning, they actually do get between him and his wife.

I guess he told me that because he thought that in some way they were like our ghost child. But I wonder if he's going to regret it.

Anyway, we staggered back to the villa as it grew rapidly lighter. At Kemal's gate, we looked at one another and neither of us could think of anything to say. Then we hugged. He had his arms round me and I had mine round him for at least a minute. And then, without another word, he turned, went through his gate and closed it quietly behind him.

I climbed down the stairs from the road very carefully. I sat for a while at the outdoor table and looked at the view. The world was waking up. I heard Kemal shout something like 'prrrssshw' and two seconds later the grey cat shot past. It didn't so much as look at me.

As I sat there, it occurred to me that if things had been different, I might have been sitting there with Matt, neither of us saying anything, both taking in the same view. Both jumping when the cat went streaking past.

I thought about getting a book and lying in the hammock for a bit, writing off the night altogether. But then I decided it might be a good idea to get a couple of hours sleep. I didn't know what Maggie was likely to need. And, even if she was OK, I had a passing suspicion we might be called on to help Anneke and her lot.

Maggie was asleep under the mosquito net. There were no signs of strain on her face. She smelt of warmth and alcohol and dope and sweat and mosquito repellant. A pretty irresistible combination in my opinion.

Even so, I didn't want to wake her, so I snuck in next to her as quietly as someone who was as bladdered as I was could.

And it worked, she moved a little but her breathing remained regular. I wanted to put my hand on her hip, but again I didn't want to risk waking her. So I lay absolutely still, looking at the back of her head in the half light, listening to her breathing.

And then I must have fallen asleep because the next thing I knew, I was in a huge square room with a high ceiling and large windows and French doors.

There were semi-opaque drapes at each window preventing me from properly seeing what was happening outside. I suppose I could have pulled the curtains but somehow I knew that would be against the rules.

Someone must have been in the room before me and left the windows and doors open, because the drapes were shifting in what little breeze there was.

There was no furniture in the room apart from a very beautiful grand piano. Slow sad music was pouring from it even though there was no pianist. No, sad's not quite right. Melancholy, more like. But somehow ecstatic at the same time.

I know almost nothing about piano music, but in my dream I said to myself, "Ah, Schubert." And who knows? I might even have been right.

Anyway, the music seemed to exist in two layers. On top

were single notes which wandered up and down; underneath was a faster, more consistent rippling combination of notes. Chords? Melodies? I don't have the vocabulary to describe it.

But in any case it seemed that I had to listen to the music as hard as I could. Try to understand it, as if it was some kind of code. As if there was a message in it.

Maybe it was so important to focus on the music because the light was so dim in the room itself and I could hardly see through the drapes.

The world outside was a pale, grayish blur in which barely discernible shapes moved slowly and rhythmically.

They might have been clouds, they might have been trees.

I suppose they might have been camels or giant orks but it didn't seem like that sort of dream.

But even though I couldn't see outside, I somehow knew that there was a garden out there, with overgrown paths, flower beds and two beautiful twisting trees, standing up like candles, and a small ornamental fountain, its basin shaped like a sea shell.

Beyond the formal part of the garden, I knew there was an area of meadow, starred with tiny wildflowers.

And underneath the music I could just hear two sounds.

The first one seemed like the ching of metal on stone.

The other was the sound of muffled voices. I couldn't work out what anyone was saying, but they sounded like teenagers.

A bit anxious, a bit full of themselves, a bit over-excited, but basically OK.

And here's the thing: I knew that somewhere in that mix of voices was Matt's.

I couldn't pick it out—it was like trying to tune into a single voice in a large choir—but I knew that he was in there. And I knew that he was a bit anxious and bit full of himself, but I also knew that he was basically OK, too.

Twenty one grams

D r Duncan MacDougall of Haverhill, Massachusetts, a moon-faced man with a bald head and rimless glasses, is a bit of a hero of mine.

In 1907, he published a paper in *The American Journal of Medicine* entitled, *The Soul: Hypothesis Concerning Soul Substance Together with Experimental Evidence of the Existence of Soul Substance*. I love all those initial caps and the fact that he obviously enjoyed the alliterative swing of 'Soul Substance' so much that he included it twice. I can imagine him rolling the expression round his mouth as he wrote it.

The paper was an account of an experiment he had conducted back in 1901 to try to determine what happened to the body after death. MacDougall reported that it lost 'three-fourths of an ounce' at the moment of death and that—when you factored everything else out—the release of the soul from the body was the only way of accounting for this weight loss. Three-fourths of an ounce is twenty one grams.

Working in an old people's home, Dr MacDougall constructed a special bed on delicately calibrated platform beam scales. Six patients in the very last stages of their life were placed in this bed and weighed. They were then weighed again at the precise moment they died. The experiment was witnessed by four other doctors.

I have read his paper so many times that I can quote chunks of it from memory. Speaking of one of his patients, MacDougall wrote: "*The instant life ceased the opposite scale pan fell with a suddenness that was astonishing—as if something had suddenly been lifted from the body.*"

He repeated the experiment with fifteen dogs and was unable to detect any weight change—thus proving to his own satisfaction that dogs don't have souls.

Not surprisingly, MacDougall's findings divided opinion. A fellow physician, Augustus P Clarke, swiftly rubbished his findings. Clarke argued that body temperature actually rises *post mortem* because the lungs are no longer cooling the blood. This can lead to sweating and that evaporation of sweat could account for the twenty one grams. To boost his argument, he pointed out that dogs don't have sweat glands so that it was scarcely surprising that their weight didn't change after death.

It's hard to believe that these guys were serious.

But whatever you make of Clarke's critique, even a cursory reading of MacDougall's paper raises major problems.

Turns out that although he conducted the experiment on six patients, only one of them yielded the results he was looking for.

Of the other five, two had to be excluded from his results for 'technical reasons'. In one case, the patient inconveniently died within moments of being placed on the bed, while MacDougall was still adjusting the beam. In the other, MacDougall was unable to conduct the experiment properly because of 'a good deal of interference by people opposed to our work'. Intriguing, huh?

Of the remaining three, one showed a drop in weight which then reversed itself (had the soul decided it preferred things in the body?) and two showed weight drop followed a few moments later by a further drop (had these individuals died twice?)

In one of these cases the initial weight drop did not occur until at least a minute after death. MacDougall explained this by saying that since the patient had been slow and 'phlegmatic' in life it was hardly reasonable to expect their soul to be any quicker off the mark in its dash for the infinite.

So, pretty much a load of old rubbish really.

Even so, it seems to me that his response to the fact of death is no worse than many others. Certainly, after Matt, I found his work consoling—precisely because of its absurdity. For a while, I sought out every crazy theory of death: spiritualism, theosophy, anthroposophy. They seemed to be fumbling towards an understanding of the awfully big adventure in ways that seemed more appropriate than all the reasoned guff about magical thinking and the psychology of loss. It wasn't that I could buy into their bonkers theories. It was more that I was in sympathy with the way they were so obviously floundering around.

Confronted by the great mystery of death, its utter unaccountability, its refusal to give up its secrets, MacDougall tried in his daft way to solve the mystery, to retrieve its secrets, to account for it. And he did it the only way he knew how, by trying to measure it. After all, in his world, what could be measured could be explained.

His ideas may have come from left field of left field, but I have a sneaking admiration for them. And if I thought for a moment that I could believe in the existence of a soul, I'd jump at the chance.

Just thinking about this bonkers old medic and his bizarre experiments made me smile at a time when there didn't seem to be much else to smile about.

And speaking of smiling, when I woke this morning—having slept amazingly well all things considered—Steve was still fast asleep with this dopey smile on his face. I put my arm round him and he said, "The radishes really do look marvelous on the shelf." I wasn't about to argue. Indeed, I was happy to take his word for it. So I left him to it.

I had this sense that something had changed in me. I felt lighter, freer, more in control of my thoughts and feelings. Last night must have been tough on Anneke and Kemal, but it seems as if it did me some good. Anyway, it's Anneke's fault for making us smoke all that dope.

I still have this image—a freeze frame really—in my head of Kemal in mid leap, his bits and pieces on display, just before he hit the water with an almighty crash. A twenty-first century Bacchus. A portly lord of excess and misrule. It makes me want to laugh but, even so, it's an image that I'm hoping won't stay with me too long. But then, I'm one to talk. What must Steve and I have looked like to Anneke? We probably traumatized the poor girl. She certainly knows now, if she didn't before, what the future holds.

Anyway, now that I was up, I had a long hot shower and washed my hair. I scrubbed myself all over, even cleaned between my toes which I usually can't be bothered with. Then I brushed my hair, put on a clean skirt and T shirt, and dabbed on a spot of lippy. I looked at myself in the mirror. Not exactly Michelle Pfeiffer, but not too ghastly (as long as I half closed my eyes).

I made a pot of coffee and took it to the table outside. The air was warm and as soft as an embrace. The sun was already up and everything looked clear and sparkling, as if I was looking at the landscape through a magnifying glass. The coffee was delicious and I realized that I didn't have the least hangover.

There was a rustling in the bushes to my right and the grey cat appeared. It climbed cautiously onto the chair beside me, knowing I wouldn't chase it away. It didn't seem to want any food. I felt honoured that something as wild as this (and you don't get much wilder than a feral cat) would trust me and want to be with me. I rubbed its head and it closed its eyes and produced a broken, not entirely convincing purr.

And then I sat there waiting to see what would happen next.

What happened next was that a jay sat on a branch of the pine tree in front of me, sparkling in the sun. And then it was chased away in a flurry of feathers by a golden squirrel with huge Alberts. The squirrel sat on the branch munching a pine cone as if it didn't have a care in the world. And maybe it didn't. Apart from transporting its unfeasibly large genitalia with it wherever it went, of course. (In spite of myself, I had a sudden flash-back of Kemal dive bombing us, arse forwards.)

And speaking of genitalia, the next thing that happened was that Steve appeared at the door and slumped into the chair at the head of the table. The cat raised one eyelid but decided to risk staying where it was. And it had obviously calculated right, because for the first time Steve didn't try to chase it away. He simply ignored it. I poured him some coffee and asked what he'd been dreaming about.

He said that he couldn't remember much, although he thought it might have had something to do with piano music.

"And not just any old piano music, *classical* piano music. My dreams seem to be getting classier in my old age."

I knew that there was something that he wasn't telling me, but I didn't press it. After all, it's likely enough that he was dreaming about Matt, and I can see why he wouldn't want to get into all that again. On the other hand, he might equally have been dreaming of Anneke naked in the moonlight, and I wouldn't necessarily want to know that even if I can easily understand it. I guess he's entitled to go where he wants in his dreams. So, all in all, probably best not to bring the matter up.

The fourth thing that happened (if you exclude eating breakfast which wasn't very exciting) was that I went to see Anneke.

"Good morning, Maggie, you look nice."

"Hi, Anneke. Listen, do you mind if we *don't* talk about last night? *Not ever.* It's all so enormous that if I start pouring out my heart to you, there's no telling when I would be able to stop. Can we just pretend that nothing happened? Go on as before? I promise not to mention Matt again."

Anneke looked very relieved and I could hardly blame her.

"Yes, of course," she said. And then she said, "Did something happen last night? I drank so much and smoked so much that I can't remember much about it. I can't even remember how the kids and I got home."

She was joking, of course... At least, I'm almost sure that she was joking.

"Now, where are those kids of yours? Maybe I can help you get them some breakfast."

"They are still asleep. Perhaps we should have just a little smoke before we wake them. What do you think?"

Goddess

I don't know how long I've been here. It could be an hour. It could be a day, a week, a year or a hundred years. I know that I am lying on grass and I can feel the sun, hot on my face. I want to go on lying here. Never move again. Disappear into the ground like the Lycians and their cities. Or dry to a husk, turn to dust and be blown away on the wind like the body in the rock tomb.

If I could come up with a single memory of a time before last week, I think I could be satisfied. It would at least indicate that I had a life, however brief. But there's nothing. I can't even remember Mum ever being younger. The only face I know is her face now. The face of a middle-aged woman. A face that can't quite hide its tiredness and sadness. I've been searching my memory for a picture of a younger woman, her face lit up by her joy in a child. I can't find it.

My eyes may be closed but I can see the blood in my eyelids. I can feel it pulsing there. I can see cells floating across my retina. I can feel the hair on my arms touched by the air. I'm aware of my heart beating. Conscious of my breathing. In... and out. In... and out. I can feel my liver and my kidneys and my spleen. I can feel my digestive system working, even though I guess I've never eaten anything. I can feel the neurons whizzing around in my brain, synapses crackling.

How can I experience myself so intensely and still not be real? How can I see so much, touch so much, feel so much, smell so much—every single minute of every day—if none of this is real?

I know it before I hear it. There's someone else in the garden. I don't want to deal with this. They're standing over me. I know that it's Ali. But, I don't want to share my misery with him. I don't want him to share his with me.

I can feel him squat down beside me. He touches my shoulder, "Matt?"

To my surprise, that touch is massively important to me. I can feel him and he can feel me. We both exist for each other, if for no one else. That moment when his hand rested on my shoulder has worked a kind of magic. I *can* still feel. I *can* still feel real.

I open my eyes but the light is so bright that I am momentarily dazzled. Ali is between me and the sun. A light burns around the edge of him.

As I'm gradually able to focus, I can see his face more clearly. His eyes are red and swollen. He has been crying. And I feel an aching sorrow, a sorrow for him so deep and so endless that it is bigger even than the sorrow I feel for myself. After all, he had something to lose, a life to lose, memories of a time before. I make an effort and sit up. How can it be so hard to sit up if nothing is real? How is it that gravity still applies? How is it that my muscles can still stiffen? My eyes hurt in bright light?

I put my arm on Ali's shoulder. Neither of us says anything for a while.

Finally, Ali says, "I could not understand why my father was so old. Why the sight of me made tears to his eyes. I said I was sorry. I felt I had done wrong. He said seeing me was the best thing that had happened since... And then he stopped. He did not wish to continue. I asked him, 'Since what, beloved Baba?' And he would not or could not answer. There were many tears on his face. I think he wished to embrace me but he did not come near. Again I asked him and then he said that he was more happy in that moment than since I had died. That I had been dead for many, many years and that he had spent those years in grief for me. He had not thought to see me again."

As he reaches this point in his story, Ali covers his face with his hands and weeps silently. I want to comfort him but I can think of no words that will penetrate his sorrow, no words that might take away his terrible grief.

Then he says, "You show no surprise at the things I am saying. Did you know this?"

I say that I did, but I could not find the words to tell him. That he seemed so busy and happy with his digging that I could not bring myself to break the spell. That I did not know that things would turn out in the way that they have.

Ali pauses for a moment and then continues, "At first I could not believe his words. I thought he was punishing me for something and yet his face was so sad. I asked him how I had died... Again, he did not want to answer. Again I asked him. Then he said, 'You fell my son. I think you must have found the rock tomb or perhaps you were just searching for birds' eggs. When you didn't come home that evening, I searched everywhere for you. In my panic I asked for the support of my neighbours —Yannis, Mazhar and Sefik—to join the search. Do you remember them? They are old men now. Yannis found your body. He carried you home as the day was fading. I have always blamed myself. All these years I have thought that it would not have happened if I had spent more time with you, if I had been a better father. But I was so busy with my work and my studies. I did not leave enough time for you. I allowed my career and dusty scholarship and my grief for your mother to come between us. And I was never able to make amends.'"

Ali says, "I told him this was not so. That he was best of fathers. He had always shared his studies with me as soon as I was of an age to understand. I said I loved and respected him. That he was both father and mother to me."

Again he weeps.

"But then", says Ali, "I knew it was time to leave. Time to come back to this garden. Time to find my friend. I wanted to stay with my father but knew that I could not. I said that I would return if I could. As I turned to go, he said, 'Even if you cannot return I will always be grateful for this visit. My heart will always be yours.' He looked so sad, but I knew that I could not stay. That my place was with you."

We sit together as the sun climbs in the sky and the day gets ever hotter. The air dances around us. I can feel every molecule in motion. I can feel the light that breaks on us as both wave and particle. I feel more alive than ever before.

Eventually, Ali wipes his eyes and sits up straighter, "And how are things with you my friend?"

"Like you, Ali, I am a ghost." I cannot say to him that I am nothing.

"This I know. This I have always known. When first I saw

you—when you came to me here in this garden—I *was* afraid. I thought you were spirit sent to protect it. But after first minute I knew there was nothing to fear. I knew we would be friends."

He pauses for a while. "And did you visit your mother and father after we parted yesterday?"

I don't want to talk about that. I don't want to admit that I envy him. That in some ways he has so much more than me. That he had a life and still exists in his father's memory. But then I remember that Ali's father has been dead for so many years and that his house in the hills is a ruin, all his scholarship has been forgotten, his neighbours are dead or moved away.

So perhaps Ali does not have so very much more than me, after all.

A bird that I have heard once before is singing its single, urgent note from the top of one of the trees like flames—Tssit. Tssit. Tssit.

"Listen to that bird," I say to Ali.

Tssit. Tssit. Tssit.

It makes Ali smile and I realize that I'm smiling too. I never thought that this would happen again.

"Shall we do some more digging?" I say.

Ali smiles again.

We move to a different point of the garden, somewhere we have never dug before. We clear away the scrub and use Ali's trowel to break through the baked topsoil.

Another bird joins the song of welcome: Tssit. Tssit. Tssit. And then another and another. Birdsong fills the air. Somehow the mingling of those single notes creates a melody. It's like the song the waves make when they whisper on the shore. Or the music of the olive trees as they surge and sway and retreat in the wind. It is the music trapped inside a seashell. The music of sap rising in trees. The music of rocks baking in the sun.

Ali digs with his trowel and I lift the soil out with my hands. Even when we have dug a deep hole the earth still feels warm in my palms and under my fingernails. (How can I feel the pressure of dirt under my nails and not be real?) In spite of my terror and loneliness, the soil feels warm and familiar.

Suddenly Ali stops. And in that moment I see it too.

At the bottom of the hole, looking up at us out of the multicoloured dirt is a single tiny eye. White and unwinking.

We stare at it and it stares back at us.

My mouth is suddenly dry. It is as if I have dreamed this moment. Both Ali and I use our hands to scrape away the surrounding dirt and the eye becomes a small clay head which, as we continue to dig, becomes a glazed clay figure maybe ten or twelve centimetres high.

We lift her—and she is very obviously a her—carefully out of the hole. Her breasts are bare but she's wearing a full skirt that covers her legs and feet. One of her arms is missing. The other is outstretched and in her hand she is holding something long and thin: a snake, a knife? Perched on the top of her head is what looks like an animal but it's so badly eroded that it's impossible to say for sure what it is—an owl maybe, some kind of cat? How strange is that? Her head and upper body are plain terracotta—apart from two white dots for her eyes, highlighted by two black, arched eyebrows. A number of wavy black lines have been painted down her skirt to make it look like pleats in material.

Alexander's Dream

Ali says that he has seen pictures of objects like this in his father's books. He thinks she may be Minoan. That she may have been made in Crete years before the Lycian settlement here was even thought of. He thinks she might be a fertility goddess. But what can she be doing here?

"She may have been offering to the gods. A gift left at a shrine. My father says that although Minoan civilization was at beginning of time, it was best time and place to live in all human history. He says Minoans must have thought they were in paradise. We remember them in the myths of Atlantis, the drowned civilization."

He hands her to me. My fingers are trembling. As soon as I touch her, I can feel her force, her magic. Tiny though she is, she's an object of incredible power. So much power that I'm amazed that the skin of my hand isn't sizzling. That she hasn't burnt an imprint of herself on my palm.

In this single moment I can feel all of her four thousand year history passing through my brain. I see (from above) an island burning in the sun. I see shining palaces with pillars painted red and yellow; terraces, fountains and baths; crowds in beautiful robes of white and purple and scarlet; paintings on the walls of monkeys and flying fish and pheasants. I hear the sounds of battles, the smell of blood and burning timber, the blare of trumpets. I see men with the heads of bulls. Acrobats in a ring. I grope my way through an underground maze. I feel the earth shake and shift. I am in the darkness of a ship's hold. I hear the timbers creak as the ship muscles its way forward. I see a wave that grows to a terrifying height; a wave that blocks the sun before it slowly unfolds, devouring the whole world.

235

All this happens in an instant and is gone. What remains is the sense of this figure's power and its intense longing to move back though time and space to where and when she came from.

Tssit. Tssit. Tssit.

Nebuchadnezzar's palace

Babylon. June 323BC. Alexander is dying in the old palace of Nebuchadnezzar on the west bank of the Euphrates. He has been running a fever for ten days. He attempted to get cooler by drinking unmixed wine and sleeping on the marble floor of his blue-tiled bathroom. But that just seems to have made everything worse.

This morning, they picked him up and carried him to his bed. Sponged him down. Such a thing has never happened before. He knows that he will not get up again. He has asked to be buried at Siwa, but he suspects that they won't do it. He has asked that his hands should be left loose, hanging free from his coffin for all to see. His point is that even the greatest go out of the world empty handed and that the only real treasure is time. But he suspects that they won't do that either. He slips in and out of consciousness, in and out of dreams. He is thirty two years old.

Maybe he should never have come. Maybe he should have heeded the omens. The priests had begged him not to enter the city, warned that evil might befall him. He had tried to evade his destiny by entering through a rear gate. A few days later, a tame ass attacked the largest and fiercest lion in his private zoo and kicked it to death. Given Alexander's lifelong identification with lions, this was a disaster. And then, while he was sailing in the marshes, his diadem had blown off and snagged in the reeds. A sailor with an eye to the main chance had dived in to recover it and returned to the boat with it on his head to keep it out of the water. Alexander's initial response had been to reward him with a talent of silver. But, after consultation with his seers, he had him executed. Well, it suddenly seemed like the right thing to do. After all, once he'd had time to think about it, it was obvious that anyone else wearing his crown had to be the worst possible news.

In his waking moments he is aware of them all crowding round him. His generals—Ptolemy, Seleucus, Eumenes, Perdikkas; his admiral, Niarchos; terrified physicians, courtiers, slaves. He has never been able to take a solemn moment entirely seriously and even now he has to stifle the urge to laugh.

He knows that their loyalty to him is, as it has always been, absolute. But he also knows that they have no loyalty to each other and that when he is gone they will tear apart the world he has made.

When they begged him to name a successor, he said that that his empire should go '*hoti to kraitisto*'—to the strongest. He never could resist the temptation to create a moment, even though he knew as he said it that it was bound to end in tears. After all, there is only one way to prove who is the strongest. And now he is unable to speak and could not retract what he has said even if he wanted to.

For the first time in his life he allows himself the luxury of a backward glance. He has come such a long way: Turkey, Syria, Lebanon, Israel, Egypt, Iraq, Iran, Afghanistan, Pakistan and India. To the world's end and half way back. He knows that he will never see Macedonia again.

He thinks of the fabled cities he has entered in triumph: Xanthus, Tyre, Babylon, Gaza, Persepolis, Oxiana, Samarkand.

In the past decade, he has founded cities and commanded an army that has consistently punched way, way above its weight. At the oasis at Siwa the oracle of Zeus declared him the son of God. At Issus he defeated Darius's cavalry in a cloud of dust. At Memphis, under the laconic gaze of a newly carved Sphinx with a perfect nose and a young girl's complexion, he was enthroned as Pharaoh. At Susa on the Mesopotamian plain, he plundered forty thousand talents of silver from the treasury, not to mention gold and jewels. (While there, he searched for but could not find a life-sized golden statue of Apollo.) In the Oxus desert he marched his soldiers to safety at night, the heat of the day being unendurable. In the foothills of Kashmir he took possession of the city of Sangada, previously the territory of a local satrap famed for his particularly large elephants. At Multan, 'city of gold' in the southern Punjab, he survived being shot with a poisoned arrow, before his men—seeing their commander had fallen—stormed the city. And so on and so on and so on. And all before his thirty third birthday.

Certainly, there are less impressive CVs.

The faces of the people he has loved pass before him.

Hephaestion, of course, the love of his life—'He too is Alexander'. Who drank himself to death in Ecbatana, just as his beautiful face was beginning to coarsen. Of the hundreds of thousands of deaths Alexander has seen, that one caused him the greatest agony. He had no idea how to respond, simply didn't have the appropriate emotional equipment.

First, he had his friend's doctor, Glaucias, put to death for incompetence, banned the playing of flutes and ordered that all horses' manes and tails should be docked.

But when this didn't mitigate his grief, he razed the temple of Asclepius, the god of medicine, to the ground.

And when this also failed, he resorted to spectacle, to gigantism. Built a funeral pyre three times the height of the tallest tree, with gilded figures of eagles, centaurs, bulls, lions and serpents, at a cost of more than twelve thousand talents. Such a conflagration would ensure that no particle of his friend's earthly body could survive; would guarantee that his spirit was unencumbered. Free to roam. The walls of the city had to be insulated to protect them from the heat of the flames and prevent them cracking.

Then there is Sisygambis, Queen Mother of Persia, more than twice Alexander's age, tall, unbending, contemptuous of her own son's cowardice.

Alexander called her mother in public but visited her rooms at night. In spite of their determination to keep the relationship a secret, rumours started to leak out almost immediately. He always said that he felt most mortal, least godlike, when he was asleep or during sex. Sisygambis, the mother of one king and the lover of another, was the exception who proved the rule.

His lack of interest in Darius's sister-wife Stateira was interpreted as chivalry, as evidence of his iron self-discipline. The truth was that, in Alexander's eyes, she could not hold a candle to the older woman. (On learning that Alexander has died, Sisygambis will seal herself in her room, turn her face to the wall and starve herself to death.)

There is Roxana, daughter of a Sogdian mountain chief, most beautiful woman in the world, pregnant with the child he will never see. Rather than claim her by right of conquest, he asked for her hand in marriage. At their wedding, he sliced a loaf in two with his sword and handed her half.

There is Bagoas his eunuch slave, his Persian boy.

And there is Bucephalus, as black as pitch, already twelve years old—only a year younger than the prince himself—when Alexander first tamed him. The most expensive horse in history. Bucephalus, who never tolerated another rider on his back and who died of old age in India, a world away from the Thessalian pastures where he gambolled as a foal.

But even as he reviews the things he has seen and done, his mind keeps returning to those first early months in Asia. Those first few steps on a lifetime's journey. Back when his successes were not tainted with an inevitable sense of disappointment.

He finds that he can remember everything. How the bull they slaughtered on the deck of his flagship as an offering to Poseidon as they crossed the Hellespont struggled and bellowed. How its eyes rolled in terror. Holding a golden bowl under its throat while its hot blood splashed up his forearms and on his chest. Hurling the bowl into the sea to ensure that the nereids were onside.

He remembers the glories of the Lycian coast, with its densely forested mountains and its cliffs tumbling into the shining, wine-dark sea. Its bears and wolves. Its soaring eagles and speeding hawks. Its one usable road hugging the shoreline. The neither-one-thing-nor-another of the coastal marshes, where the reeds danced continuously, reminding him of home.

He savours the memory of disbanding his fleet at Miletus. That was another of his moments. He knew that he was astonishing posterity, but the truth of the matter was that he didn't have enough money to maintain it.

All that autumn, he worked his way southwards and eastwards. Many cities opened their doors to him, others mistakenly held out. It was all one and the same. One after another, the mountain fastnesses and coastal strongholds fell to him.

He had precious little free time back in those days, but once he and Hephaestion bunked off for a day to do a little desultory hunting. They rose at dawn and took just the one dog between them. There were no boars in the forest that day but they found themselves in a densely wooded gorge at the bottom of which a swirling river flowed westward into the sea. Peregrines flickered across the sky, bees zoomed in the shade, trout sparkled in black pools. The going was rough but they followed the gorge downwards finally arriving, hours later, filthy and scratched, at a small cove with a sandy beach. Even though it was late in the year, the sea was warm. After they had swum, they lay on the sand and watched the sun set behind two small islands, one with twin humps like a camel. In the glitter of the sun on the water, the islands seemed to be floating in the sky. For a moment, Alexander came close to forgetting that he was in the business of conquering worlds.

He and Hephaestion slept that night on the sand, wrapped in their cloaks, while the dog snored at their feet. They returned to camp the next day to find everything in uproar, search parties being formed.

A few days later, Alexander sent home on leave all the Macedonian soldiers who had been married in the months before the start of the campaign.

And onwards, south and east.

In his delirium he again remembers the dream he had the night before his visit to the Didymaion, before the god gave him a foretaste of what was to come. The faces of the two boys are as clear to him as those of Sisygambis and Hephaestion and the others. He has never forgotten them. He has dreamed them a number of times in the intervening years.

Always the same dream: one boy falling; the other in danger of falling.

He has not told Aristander of these repeated dreams. He knows that their meaning is hidden from the seer—now a frail old man who spends most of his life asleep—and he did not wish to see him fail again in his interpretations.

When he wakes from this dream he is always haunted by a sense of his own helplessness. That he ought to have been able to save them.

He remembers that when he and Hephaestion were working their way through the gorge to the sea, there was something familiar about the sheer rock faces that hemmed them in on both sides. He had the sense that he had been here before, but that was clearly impossible. For hours the idea nagged at him, until he realized it was a landscape he had seen in his dreams. When he looked up, he almost expected to see the boys balancing on the edge of the cliff, high above him. And, in that moment, he thought he *did* see a figure standing just above the point at which a huge fig tree grew out of the rock face. He raised his arm as if in a salute. But it must have been the heat of the afternoon because when he cleared the sweat from his eyes and looked again, there was no one there. Just the sunlight flashing on the fig tree's leaves.

He knows that he is failing fast. He knows that he can count the hours that remain to him on the fingers of his two hands. He has no energy to protest. Besides, going like this answers the question of what he is to do with the rest of his life. All that remains for him is to die well.

A slave wipes his face with a cloth dipped in rosewater. He opens his eyes for a moment, registers the fear and pity in the woman's eyes and then sinks into unconsciousness where the boys are waiting for him.

First one and then the other is silhouetted at the top of the cliff. Again, Alexander waves. This time, however, they both wave back. The first boy does not fall. Somehow he knows that the second boy is in no danger. He can see that they are speaking to one another and then, as if they have made up their minds, they scramble fearlessly down the cliffside, like goats. Pebbles scatter under their feet and rattle down the rocks.

The boys are now on level ground. Slowly they walk towards Alexander who is waiting for them, unable to move. They stop in front of him and smile shyly. The slighter of the boys has his hand over his eyes to protect them from the sun. The older boy approaches Alexander and touches his wrist. A shock runs all the way from Alexander's heart to the place that the boy touched. The boy says something but Alexander can't hear it. And then they turn and walk away from him, away from the cliff. As they go, they start to lose shape and definition. They blur at the edges, they start to dissolve. But before they disappear altogether, they stop once more and then turn back to Alexander. They beckon him to join them.

Alexander is flooded with joy that is like a kind of paralysis. That gesture is what he has been waiting for all his life. It is the last thing he sees.

Alexander's generals noted that even as his fever was at its most intense, as his brain was boiling, and as the eunuchs around his bed began their unearthly cries of woe, Alexander continued to smile...

... ...
... ...

... ...
... ...

...

Maybe it happened like that.
Maybe it didn't.

To the elements be free

Steve: Typical. Maggie waited until the plane was in the air before she told me that she'd invited Anneke and her kids to come to stay with us in London. Total bastard *numero due* is also invited, although Maggie thinks it is unlikely that he will turn up. As the plane banked over the shining sea and headed back inland I knew—I just *knew*—that Anneke will be on our doorstep within a couple of weeks, with no money to pay the taxi driver who has brought her and the kids from the airport. As we turned north and started to climb, I further realized that I was looking forward to it.

Kemal: When Maggie and Steve left this afternoon, they seemed OK. Amid the goodbyes, they promised to come back next year. I'm not sure what I think about that. In fact there are quite a few things I'm not sure what I think about. I feel like I've been to some very strange places in the last few days. Some of it has been fun (seeing Anneke naked, for example). Some of it has made me feel guilty (smoking drugs). And some of it both felt like fun and a guilty secret at the same time (my nakedness as I hit the water). Seyhan will be back in a couple of days. It's clear that her mother is not going to die. Seyhan and I will have time together. I have to decide what to tell her.

Seyhan: I've just had the most extraordinary text from Kemal. He says that he is counting the hours until I return. Silly old fool. He also said that as there are no guests scheduled for next week, perhaps we should move into the villa and make use of the pool. And, if I'm reading him right, he seems to be suggesting that we could swim naked, at least that's what I assume all his nonsense about swimming costumes being an encumbrance is getting at.

He should not get his hopes up.

When it became clear that Mother was once again going to confound expectations and not die, her doctor and the staff at the home were astounded. I wasn't. But then, they don't know about *enargeia*. Maybe she'll find a way of living forever. If anyone can, she can.

You would think that, when one is in the presence of near death, one would think profound and important thoughts. Didn't seem to work like that. Part of me wished that she *had* died so that I wouldn't have to go on watching her life dwindling. But mainly I felt resentful that my brothers seem happy to leave this to me. The fact that I'm here with Mother always means that they are conspicuous by their absence. And I just slip back into the role of dutiful daughter. I really ought to assert myself more. Demand that they get more involved. I wonder why I don't. But I don't wonder very hard. You never know what might happen then.

Anyway, until the next time.

Maggie: I imagined a child as beautiful as a star. I dreamed a whole life for him.

Kemal: I had a glass of *çay* with old Coskun and Ilhami in the village this afternoon. Both of them were as dour as usual, in fact it's hard to imagine any two people whose names suit them less. They stopped playing backgammon just long enough to tell me that Serkan thinks someone is using his garden. Trespassing. Normally, they barely acknowledge my existence but the chance to be spiteful to one neighbour about another was too good to miss. Apparently the garden has been empty for years. Serkan knocked the old house down when his mother died. Turned off the water. It has been empty for so long because he is trying to sell it and is holding out for an absurd price. Coskun says 400,000TL. He says the man is a fool and no one will ever get that amount for just over a thousand square metres, even with all these incomers building summer villas. Serkan is apparently worried about squatters. Other people in the village have reported hearing sounds of digging coming from the garden. Serkan laid in wait for a whole day and night hoping to catch them in the act but nobody came. So, a couple of days ago, he put barbed wire across the entrance. But the digging sounds haven't stopped. Coskun and Ilhami feel that it serves him right for being so greedy. The envy in their voices was clear.

Elif: I guess Maggie means well and doesn't realize how intrusive her endless questions are. She was just talk, talk, talk. And in order to create time for more questions she did much of the cleaning herself. She denied me a role I've accepted and imposed on me one that I do not want—to pretend to be her friend. It's one thing washing and cleaning for her, quite another letting her inside my head. What I want is not kindness or conversation, but respect. And that's something I've never received from any guests.

But maybe I'm getting cold and graceless in my old age.

Urfuz says that I am becoming bitter, a shrew, that I don't

pay enough attention to him, that I don't love him. And he's right. I don't. But how can I explain that getting broadband for the kids is more important to me than he is? That it is more important than anything.

Anneke: All that with Maggie has made me think about my life and my relationship with the kids. I think I'm a pretty good mother—even that total bastard Johann would have to grant me that, even though I'm not twenty three anymore. Even so, I think I might have let things slip a bit recently. It's just so hard on your own. But never mind that. I really must clear the house up. There's rubbish all over the place. And then, when the everything's tidy, I'll take the kids to the supermarket to get the stuff for a picnic and then I'll drive them to the beach and we'll hire umbrellas so that they don't get burnt. Tonight, I'll wash their hair and cook us a proper meal and we'll eat it sitting at the table, with clean plates and knives and forks, like a proper family. And I'll drink nothing but water. But first, just a little weed.

Maggie: I imagined a child as beautiful as a star. Just a couple of days ago, I was fantasizing about how proud I would be when Anneke came to supper and met my handsome, charming boy. And how I wouldn't have minded if she'd had mildly inappropriate thoughts about him.

For two or three weeks every year I have created a series of different futures for him. One year, he could meet an English girl of his own age on the beach. So many details had to be got right. Was she pretty? Was he shy? Did her parents approve of him? Would she have supper with us? Or he might have a holiday devoted to water sports—windsurfing, sailing, swimming with turtles and dolphins, getting a PADI qualification. His skin would be baked brown, his hair blonder than ever. Another year, perhaps he would have asked if he could bring a friend along. I would have spent much of the time cooking enormous meals and dealing with smelly socks and trainers, while Steve went on about what a nightmare teenage boys were. This year, the idea came to me from somewhere that he would make friends with a Turkish boy, maybe a year or two older. They'd hang out together, talk about girls and school, maybe nick a few beers from the fridge. Half the time we wouldn't know where they were. I even had a name for him, a name that also came out of nowhere: Aydin.

Kemal: Ah, yes. That damned cat. Better deal with it before Seyhan gets back. If I see it, I'll shoot it. Otherwise, I'm sure Urfuz will help. Maybe he will find a way of poisoning it. Although he can beat it to death with a spade for all I care.

Seyhan: I wonder what Kemal's been up to while I've been away. Nothing, I imagine. Just sitting there with his English detective stories or pottering around the garden. In a way I almost wish he had been up to something. He's so middle-aged. It's years since he's taken a risk or done anything outrageous. But then I guess the same could be said of me. I know that somewhere inside that complacent exterior is the man I married. He was such a charming mix of shy and self-confident. He could always make me laugh. It's just that the old Kemal gets so few outings these days.

Urfuz: I've had a thought about the tortoise. A solution has suggested itself. If I can't kill it and it refuses to be lost, perhaps I can sell it. It is, after all, a fine big tortoise with a radiated shell. Maybe the new people who've bought the horrible pink villa on the edge of the village would be interested. A good fat tortoise might make the place feel more like home. And because the villa is surrounded by a high wall, it would not be able to escape and find its way back here to torment me. I wouldn't tell them about the shitting by the pool, of course.

Anneke: I wish that Maggie hadn't been going back to England so soon after we met. I knew as soon as I saw her that we were going to be friends. She was so simpatico. And she was so good with the children.

Steve: I wish I'd shown more enthusiasm for Agatha Christie. Kemal was obviously disappointed by my somewhat muted response. Maybe we could have discussed Lord Edgware's penchant for medieval tortures. I'll see if I can find him a nice second-hand edition when I get back to London and send it to him. Only problem is I haven't seen a second hand bookshop in years. Have no idea where the nearest one might be.

Seyhan: Part of me hasn't given up on the possibility of a medical miracle. Part of me continues to hope that the next time I come she will be sitting up in bed, perhaps reading, maybe doing some embroidery. As I come through the door, she will put whatever is in her hand on the side table and will turn to me with her arms wide and say, "Seyhan, it's you, how lovely to see you." I just can't help myself. Pathetic, huh?

Kemal: Although I am ashamed to say it, I wish I'd looked more closely at Anneke in the moonlight. After all, when am I next likely to see a naked woman under sixty? Or even one over sixty? Unless, of course, I can persuade Seyhan into a bit of skinny dipping.

Seyhan: I wish Mother had died; I wish Mother would get better.

Maggie: I imagined a child as beautiful as a star. But now I have let him go. In fact, it doesn't really feel like it's my decision to make. It's as though *he* has decided to leave *me*. It was so easy building a picture of an imaginary life. So easy to imagine how life could have been different and so hard to let him go. They say that the best things parents can do for their children is to turn them into happy, independent adults. You have to admire the ambition even if most of us are not exactly fighting our way through crowds of happy, independent adults. So, I suppose in a way all parents have to set their children free. Matt will never be an adult but what Doctor MacDougall would have described as his Soul Stuff is now able to wander wherever it wants. I remember what Prospero says when he finally releases Ariel from service: *"Then to the elements be free, and fare thou well."* Of course, we're not told what Prospero thinks, or how much he is going to miss his 'chick', how he's going to cope without him after all these years.

Still, in setting Matt free, I'm hoping to set myself free and Steve as well.

So, fare thou well, Matt…

This is where it ends…

… almost certainly.

Decision

When the people went, the woman left a bowl of food for the world's smartest cat: biscuits, chopped ham and the remains of some crumbly cheese. The cat has feasted and has been washing itself. It didn't previously have the energy. Its fur is so much more luxuriant than a week ago; the open cut on its muzzle has started to heal. The tick on its flank has also feasted and is the size of a gobstopper. As purple as a grape.

The cat has been sleeping in the shade of the house with one ear, as always, open. It has been dreaming of times of plenty, its whiskers twitching as it chases, outwits, catches and devours imaginary prey. Eventually, it uncoils itself, stretches and flickers like smoke over to the table. It swarms up the leg and hoovers up the crumbs that remain from the lunch the people ate before they left.

Then, knowing that it is alone, it settles on the table and gazes at the view, glowering contemptuously at a golden squirrel with enormous bollocks that is hanging by its feet from one of the branches in the deformed tree in front of the house. Pillock. Coming round here flaunting itself like that. It could kill it in an instant, if it could be bothered. Probably. Still, fuck old golden balls.

An orange butterfly lands on one of the chairs but the cat

doesn't pounce. A full stomach always renders it magnanimous.

It has a decision to make. And you don't get to be the world's smartest cat without thinking things through and then making the right decisions. Always.

Something is telling it that this garden may not be a good place to be in the immediate future.

So it has to choose.

Should it head down into the village and see what can be scrounged from the dustbins? Maybe it will be able to help itself to a couple of Urfuz's chickens. But that always requires a little prior risk assessment.

Or should it head back up into the hills and the forest and live in the wild for a while? (After all there will always be the option of coming back here at a later date if things get too feral.)

So, what's it to be, scrounger or hunter?

The cat sighs, leaps silently down onto the flagstones and shimmies towards the stairs. It mounts these effortlessly paw over paw, until it reaches the track behind the villa. It doesn't look back. It is not a sentimental creature.

At this moment it is planning its future and has no memory that it was ever here. No memory of the woman who allowed it to sleep against her leg or of the risible man who tried to intimidate it. No memory of the children it guarded. No memory of the old man giving it the evil eye and whispering threats. No memory of seeing a ghost.

That's in the past and the past, as every cat knows, doesn't exist.

It sits at the side of the track for a moment, still undecided. To the left, the hills; to the right, the village.

254

Its tail lashes a few times in the dust.

Then it turns left and trots watchfully along the middle of the track. It does not look back. It has never looked back in the whole of its life. It's not about to start now.

John Melmoth

NOTE

A number of Alexander's dreams are recorded, although they should all be viewed with extreme scepticism.

For example, Pliny says that Alexander was able to save his friend Ptolemaus who was dying of a poisoned wound. Alexander dreamed that a dragon was holding a medicinal plant in its mouth and told him where he could find it. Alexander found it and cured his friend and many other soldiers with it.

Another story claims that during the siege of Tyre, an island fortress, he dreamed that he was hunting in a forest with his father, back in Macedonia. Suddenly, a satyr with a splendid horse's tail appeared and started to dance wildly on a huge bronze shield on the ground. Alexander consulted Aristander who, almost two and a half thousand years before Freud, said that the dream was a kind of pun because the constituent parts of the word 'satyr' can also mean 'Tyre is thine'. The seer also claimed that the satyr's dance indicated *how* Tyre could be captured—on the ground. So, Alexander built a huge causeway and sacked the city.

Probably the most reliable account of one of his dreams relates to the spring of 332BC when he was in Egypt preparing to build the city of Alexandria. He dreamed that an old man, who he subsequently identified as Homer, came to him and recited a couple of lines from *The Odyssey* (4.395-396) about the island of Pharos. Its advantages, according to Homer, are a 'snug' harbour, a 'good' landing beach and 'dark' freshwater wells. Alexander interpreted this as architectural advice about where the new city should be situated and ordered plans to be drawn up accordingly.

So, it seems that dreams really can make things happen—even the destruction or the founding of cities—although it clearly helps if the dreamer is the unchallenged ruler of a huge chunk (more than five million square kilometres) of the known world.

Made in the
USA
Middletown, DE